D0192050

THE
BUTTON BOX

by Bridget Hodder
and Fawzia Gilani-Williams

KAR-BEN
PUBLISHING

KAR-BEN PUBLISHING®
An imprint of Lerner Publishing Group, Inc.
241 First Avenue North
Minneapolis, MN 55401 USA

Website address: www.karben.com

Cover and interior illustrations by Harshad Marathe.
Map by Laura K. Westlund.

Authors note photos: family photo courtesy of author; Umayyad Mosque photo by Moe
Huss/Shutterstock.com.

Main body text set in Bembo Std.
Typeface provided by Monotype Typography.

Library of Congress Cataloging-in-Publication Data

Names: Hodder, Bridget, author. | Gilani-Williams, Fawzia, author. | Marathe,
    Harshad, illustrator.
Title: The Button Box / by Bridget Hodder and Fawzia Gilani-Williams ; [illustrations
    by Harshad Marathe].
Description: Minneapolis, MN : Kar-Ben Publishing, an imprint of Lerner Publishing
    Group, Inc., 2022. | Includes bibliographical references. | Audience: Ages 8–13. |
    Audience: Grades 4–6. | Summary: With the help of a magic button, Jewish Ava
    and Muslim Nadeem go back in time to ancient Morocco to help Prince Abdur
    Rahman escape to Spain and fulfill his destiny as the ruler of a country in which
    Jews and Muslims will work together to make medieval Spain a center of science,
    mathematics, music, and poetry.
Identifiers: LCCN 2021008026 (print) | LCCN 2021008027 (ebook) |
    ISBN 9781728423968 | ISBN 9781728423975 (paperback) | ISBN 9781728444246
    (ebook)
Subjects: CYAC: Jews—United States—Fiction. | Muslims—United States—Fiction. |
    Cousins—Fiction. | Magic—Fiction. | Time travel—Fiction. | Jewish-Arab
    relations—Fiction. | Abd al-Rahman I, Caliph of Cordova, 731-787 or 788—
    Fiction.
Classification: LCC PZ7.1.H618 Bu 2022 (print) | LCC PZ7.1.H618 (ebook) | DDC
    [Fic]—dc23

LC record available at https://lccn.loc.gov/2021008026
LC ebook record available at https://lccn.loc.gov/2021008027

Manufactured in the United States of America
2-1009796-49346-7/14/2023

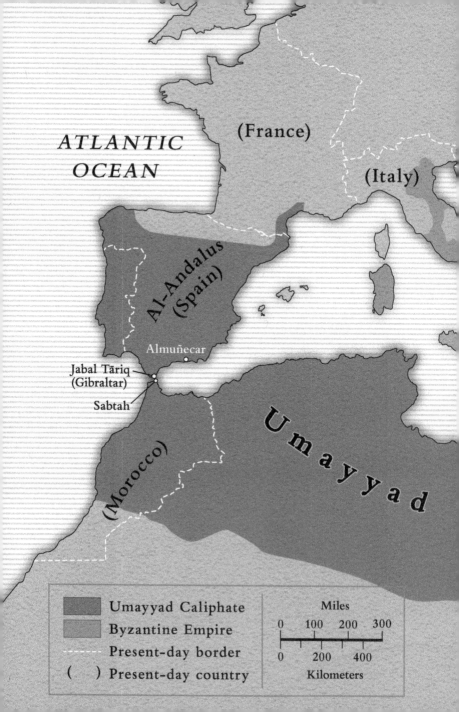

ATLANTIC
OCEAN

(France)

(Italy)

Al-Andalus
(Spain)

Almuñecar

Jabal Tāriq
(Gibraltar)

Sabtah

(Morocco)

U m a y y a d

Umayyad Caliphate

Byzantine Empire

Present-day border

( ) Present-day country

Miles
0   100   200   300

0   200   400
Kilometers

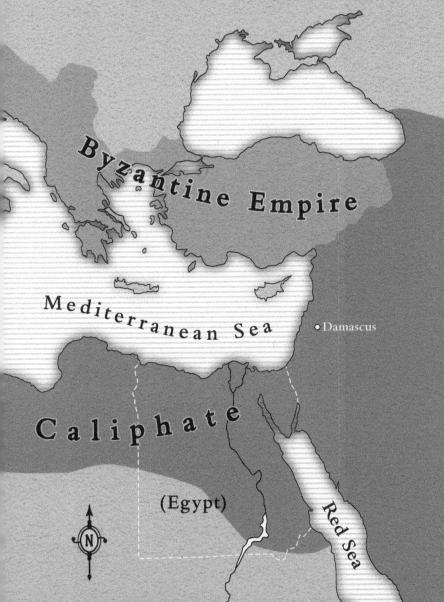

Ester ibn Evram's World:
755 CE

Byzantine Empire

Mediterranean Sea

○ Damascus

Caliphate

(Egypt)

Red Sea

N

CHAPTER 1

"Don't tell Granny Buena, okay?" Ava wiped her face on the sleeve of her sweatshirt. She hoped it wasn't obvious that she'd been crying most of the way back from school.

Her cousin Nadeem paused on the steps of their grandmother's house. She couldn't quite read the expression in his large dark eyes. This was strange, since Ava and Nadeem usually guessed each other's thoughts without having to speak a word.

"If you don't want me to say anything to Granny, I won't," Nadeem said after a pause. "But I'm going to tell my mom, so it's not as if you can keep it a secret for long anyway."

Ava knew he was right. Ever since Nadeem's dad had died a few years ago, his mom, Noora, talked to Granny pretty much every day.

"Well then, I guess we should tell her and get it over with." Ava took a deep breath and opened Granny's front door.

When they dropped their backpacks and sweatshirts in the entryway, Granny Buena appeared from the kitchen. She looked like a queen would look, Ava thought—if queens wore purple aprons. Maybe her air of elegance came from her curly silver hair, proud posture, and gleaming jewelry. Or maybe it came from something else—something deep inside. Granny welcomed Ava and Nadeem with a delighted smile that faltered when she caught the expressions on their faces.

"*La, la, la!*" Her lilting accent was kind-of-Spanish, kind-of-not. "What's wrong, *ninyos miyos?*"

Ava couldn't trust herself to speak. Instead, she made eye contact with Granny and passed an invisible mic to Nadeem.

"We're okay," Nadeem said. "But yeah—something happened today at school." He gulped, and Ava realized she wasn't the only one who felt like crying.

"Oh, my dears!" Granny opened her arms wide.

Ava flung herself into that perfumey, soft hug—which would have been a whole lot softer if Granny hadn't been wearing her usual bunch of big bumpy necklaces. Granny's hand came up to pat her hair, and the tight knot in Ava's chest began to loosen.

"Come now, children. Tell your *nona* Buena everything." Granny led them into the living room and settled onto the sofa, laying aside her purple apron and tucking in the ends of her flowing dress. She patted the cushions beside her invitingly, and the kids sat close to her on either side. "As my own grandmothers used to say: *mal de muchos, es konsuelo*," she said in a reassuring tone. "Sharing your troubles is a comfort in itself."

Ava and Nadeem were used to adults sharing quirky bits of wisdom like this. Nadeem's Muslim mom, Noora, had a traditional saying for every occasion, like "A person's tongue can give you the taste of his heart" (which made Ava wonder queasily what a heart is supposed to taste like) or "If you're a friend of the captain, you can wipe your hands on the sail" (which was just one big unanswered "Why?"). As for Granny Buena, it seemed like she couldn't go more than five minutes without quoting an old Sephardic Jewish proverb in Ladino, the language of her childhood. Ladino was a cool brew of Spanish, Hebrew, and Arabic, with a cinnamon sprinkle of Turkish.

Ava said, "If we tell you what happened, do you promise not to tell Mom? I think it will upset her."

The gentle lines of Granny's face grew serious. "Your mother is my daughter, *kerida*. Nadeem's father, rest him in peace, was my son, and his wife is now like a daughter to me. Your parents trust me to care for you after school while they're at work. Keeping something important from them would be a betrayal. It is not our way."

That was another thing Granny Buena said a lot: "It is not our way." And sometimes when Granny did things that seemed funny to Ava—like kissing leftover bread before tossing it into the compost bin—she would say, "It is our way" as a kind of non-explanation.

"Okay, then." Ava gave in with a sigh. "I'll tell you. I, uh, got into a fight with someone."

Granny arched an auburn-penciled eyebrow. "A granddaughter of mine would never do such a thing unless she had a good reason. So. Tell me what it was."

Nadeem chimed in. "There's this girl in our class—Fern. She has a problem with me being Muslim."

"And with me being Jewish," Ava added.

4

"I don't know what her deal is," said Nadeem. "We've never done anything to hurt her. But all of a sudden she's hassling us, and she won't let up."

"How exactly does Fern 'hassle' you, ninyos?"

Ava didn't want to answer, but she did. Even though it made her feel kind of sick. "She calls us names. I—I refuse to say them out loud." Those words didn't belong in her grandmother's living room. They would pollute the air.

Nadeem took a deep breath. "I'll tell her." He whispered in Granny's ear.

Granny's green eyes sparked with anger.

"Today after school," Ava explained, "Fern followed us part of the way home. She was shouting at us as usual, and . . . I guess I finally snapped. I mean, she's been on our case for weeks! So I got right in her face and yelled back. I was *this* close to shoving her. That's when Nadeem caught my wrist and stopped me." She held out her right hand. An empty thread hung from her sleeve where a white button had once been.

Nadeem grimaced. "Sorry. I didn't mean to tear off your button." He turned to Granny. "I talked Ava into leaving before we all got into a real fight. But I'm still wondering whether we should've stayed and had some kind of a showdown instead."

Granny kissed the top of Nadeem's head before he could dodge. "You did the right thing," she said. "Ah, my little birds, I wish I could hide you under my wings and shelter you from the pain of such experiences. Too many people in this world are filled with anger. They're looking for an excuse to hate someone. And unfortunately, people like us—Jews like you and me, Ava, and Muslims like you and your mother, Nadeem—have been convenient targets for people like them for a long, long time."

A voice inside Ava suddenly whispered: *Say it. Say it now!* "Something else happened today." She felt both Granny and Nadeem's gazes on her, but she kept her eyes lowered. "Nadeem, you know my friends Eliza and Rochelle? They were talking to me about you."

"Me? What did I do?" He sat bolt upright and clapped a hand on his skinny chest, his mouth hanging open. "Was it that goal I messed up in soccer last weekend?"

"No." She sighed. "Nothing like that. They've been trying to figure out a way to get Fern to stop obsessing about you and me. They told me they think we should quit hanging out together at school."

He stared. "But I thought Eliza and Rochelle liked me!"

"They do. But they said that a Muslim kid and a Jewish kid spending time together is like wearing a gigantic sign on our backs that says *Bully Us, Fern.*" Ava hung her head. She felt guilty for saying this to her cousin. But her friends had only been trying to help.

Nadeem swallowed hard. "'Do you think we should keep away from each other just because of Fern?"

Ava felt a painful wrench inside of her. "Well, maybe we could try it and see if it makes a difference. Just while we're at school."

"No!" Granny cut in sharply. "Do not give in to that notion. Ava, your friends' hearts are in the right place. But letting this problem keep you two apart is no solution, keridos. Our family may be hard to understand from the outside—especially since after your father died, Nadeem, your mother raised you as a Muslim, while Ava and her parents and I are Jewish. Yet while we have some differences, we are bound by belief in the Creator—and by our love and loyalty to each other. Nothing and nobody should break those ties." She gently hugged them both.

Ava felt relief wash over her. Granny was right.

Nadeem said, "Does this mean we can still hang out?"

Granny Buena pinched his cheek, chuckling. "You'd better!" She stood up. "Now, the time has come. My duty is clear. I shall go upstairs and look for the Button Box."

"Wait. What?" Ava blurted. Did this mean the conversation about bullying was over? Shouldn't Granny be promising to call the principal or at least talk to Fern's parents? That was what adults were supposed to do in these situations, wasn't it?

"You need a new button on your sleeve." Granny smiled at Ava's perplexed look.

Granny Buena had either suddenly lost track of the conversation, or she'd decided to move on weirdly fast. Ava might have worried that Granny was getting confused in her old age—if it hadn't been for a gleam of mischief in those wise green eyes.

She was up to something.

Granny waved a vague hand in the air. "Meanwhile, I made honey cakes. They're in the dining room. Help yourselves while you wait, and don't forget to wash your hands first."

Okaayyy . . .

Ava and Nadeem both watched curiously as Granny wafted out of the room. Trailing scarves like an elderly fairy's wings, she muttered something under her breath.

Ava caught the words of a proverb:

"En manos de mansevos, milagros."

It was one Ava had never heard before. Slowly, she translated to herself. Then she turned to Nadeem.

"In the hands of children," she said, *"there are miracles."*

CHAPTER 2

Ava and Nadeem took their places at the dining room table.

"Our *jadah*'s an awesome baker." Nadeem inhaled the delicious orange-honey scent of Granny's traditional Sephardic sponge-cake muffins. As he grabbed one from the serving dish, he said "*Bismillah*" and sank his teeth into it. Ava knew this meant "in the name of God" in Arabic. He said it a lot, and always before eating. "These are what people must have snacked on before there were Twinkies."

"Oh, please. Twinkies are gross."

Ava felt a smooth, furry head knock against her knee. Their grandmother's gold Abyssinian cat jumped into her lap. "Sheba! Hello there, sweetie." She petted the purring creature. "Where have you been, huh? Were you hiding from our drama?"

Nadeem gave a kind of snort-laugh. "You treat Sheba like she's human. You'd never, ever catch me talking to a cat."

"Aw, come on," said Ava. "How can you not adore the super-adorable Sheba?" The cat reached up and caught the tiny tip of a claw in one of Ava's light-brown curls. Ava giggled and untangled it. "Yes, kitty, I'm talking about you."

Nadeem shrugged and swallowed another bite of cake. "You know I'm just not that into cats. But I guess if you have to have one, Sheba's okay." Then his gaze sharpened. "Hey . . . what's that shiny orange thing hanging from her collar?" He reached for it, but the cat drew back.

Ava bent over Sheba and looked closer. Dangling from the cat's collar was a jewel, like the ones pampered fluffy kittens wore on pet-food cans. "How pretty! I guess Granny bought her a new collar. But this jewel can't be real, right? It's too fabulous."

At that moment, Granny Buena reappeared, holding a black velvet bundle in both hands. "Of course Sheba's jewel is real," she said as though Ava had been talking to her. "It's a fire opal. In our family, many things are possible that might seem impossible."

"Whoa," was all Nadeem could say.

Ava blurted, "That must have cost a lot!"

"I didn't buy it, kerida," Granny said with a chuckle. "She's always worn that collar. Cats in our family have worn the fire opal from generation to generation, for hundreds of years."

A tingle went down Ava's arms. This was one of the things she loved most about spending time with her grandmother—the sentences that started or ended with those words: "for hundreds of years." Then she paused to wonder. If Sheba had always been wearing the opal, why had she and Nadeem never noticed it before?

Granny placed the velvet bundle on the dining table. "Now, my darling grandchildren, allow me to introduce you to . . . the Button Box." She tugged at the wrapping, which fell away to reveal an extraordinary object. It was a box made of clear crystal, rising up on four legs that were a rosy copper color. The lid was bound and hinged with the same metal. Along the shining sides of the box, elegant symbols were painted in glimmering gold. For a second, the air around it seemed to shimmer like glitter exploding from a popped glue tube.

Wow!

This wasn't at all what Ava had expected. She leaned forward and picked it up with both hands. It was very heavy. The small items inside shifted and sparkled, clinking like treasure in a pirate's chest.

"That's so cool!" Nadeem cried.

"Our family has saved buttons in this box for perhaps a thousand years," said Granny. "In fact, my dears, some of them are so old that they aren't really buttons at all."

Ava's arms were getting tired. She gently put the fantastic box down. "I guess I never really thought about there being a time before buttons were invented."

"Can I hold the Button Box?" Nadeem reached out.

Granny smiled. "Yes, but be careful. It's ancient. And there are many stories locked inside."

Sheba the cat leaped onto the table. She curled her long gold body and dark-tipped tail around the crystal container.

"There, there, Sheba. The children will be gentle with it," Granny Buena said. "Right, Nadeem?"

Nadeem nodded with an embarrassed look. Ava figured he was remembering how he'd knocked a water glass off the table and into Granny's lap last week. Sometimes his elbows and arms seemed to have minds of their own. "I'll be extra careful."

As if she'd understood, Sheba relaxed, approached Nadeem, and gave him an encouraging nudge. Then she turned and nosed at the cake crumbs on Ava's plate.

Ava shooed her off. "Granny, what did you mean about stories being locked inside the box?" she asked.

Granny's smile widened. "Each button guards the tale of the ancestor who wore it." She gently lifted the lid and dug around inside. "Aha. Here's a remarkable one!"

She pulled out a silver oval and held it high. It was covered with twirly patterns and tiny, winking red stones that looked like rubies.

Ava gasped. "That's a *button*?"

"It was used like a button, but perhaps it's more accurate to call it a pin. This belonged to your long-ago ancestor, Ester ibn Evram. She was a fine lady in the court of the Muslim ruler Abdur Rahman the First, in medieval Spain. But she started out as a spice seller in a North African marketplace."

Whoa. Ava wondered why she'd never heard any of this before. She wasn't too clear on what medieval Spain was either.

"Do you mean *the* Abdur Rahman?" Nadeem cried, dropping his fourth orange-honey cake onto his plate. "I was named after him!"

"Your name is Nadeem," Ava pointed out helpfully.

He looked like he might have stuck his tongue out at her if he were just a smidgen less proud of how mature he was these days. "Okay, genius, what's my middle name?"

"Ab—abdul—?"

"Abdurahman," he said, leaving the *so there* unspoken. "He was a famous prince in, um, ancient times. Is that who you're talking about, Granny?"

Granny nodded. "Of course. Abdur Rahman the First and his family honored our Jewish ancestors in old Spain. We worked together, Jews and Muslims, to pursue knowledge when the rest of Europe was still in the Dark Ages. Our astronomers mapped the stars. Our doctors invented the first true forms of surgery. Our libraries were the greatest in the world. Together, we made Spain a center of science, mathematics, music, and poetry."

She said *we* as if Granny, Ava, and Nadeem had actually been there in person. Ava found herself thinking that history was way more fascinating when you were connected to the ones who made it.

"Just think, Ava," Granny went on. "Abdur Rahman became a great leader while he was only about as old as your tutor."

Ava's tutor was a guy named Theo. He came over to her parents' house once a week to help Ava with her terrible spelling. He had a small, strange beard. He studied film at the university a few blocks away where Ava's dad worked. Theo couldn't even reheat a pizza correctly, much less lead Spain.

"Amazing," she said.

Granny handed her the silver pin. Ava wasn't sure why, but her heart began to beat faster.

Nadeem bounced in his chair. "Can you believe our great-great-great-grandmother, or whatever she was—the spice seller—knew Abdur Rahman the First, the guy I'm named after? What a coincidence!"

"Coincidence is simply fate in disguise," Granny Buena remarked.

Nadeem gazed down at the pin in Ava's hand. He ran his fingertip over the complex design and the red stones. Then he whipped his head to one side. "Hey. Do you hear that humming sound?"

"Yeah." Ava glanced around, trying to figure out where it was coming from. What a strange noise! Almost like lots and lots of whispering voices. There was music in the sound too—a little like the songs she sang with her parents and Granny on the Sabbath at Temple Beth-El.

"I think it's coming from the button!" Nadeem moved closer.

Just as Ava leaned her head down to check, Granny Buena reached over with her long fingers and snatched the button away.

The humming stopped.

Nadeem gave a startled squeak.

"Granny!" Ava cried. "What was that? Didn't you hear it?"

"Never mind, my dears," Granny said casually. She returned the silver pin to the Button Box. "First things first. Weren't we going to mend your shirt, Ava? Let's find the extra button I saved for your sleeve."

"But, Granny . . ." Nadeem objected.

She didn't seem to hear him. "Where is that pesky piece of plastic?" she muttered as she searched through the box. "It should be right on top. I didn't even mean to keep it here in the first place—I should have put it in my sewing box. Aha!" She retrieved a small, white, heart-shaped button. "Found it. Let's sit in the living room and sew this back on, ninyos."

17

"Hold on a minute," Ava insisted. "What just happened when Nadeem touched that pin?"

Granny gave one of her elegant shrugs, almost like a move from ballet. "Nothing has happened. At least not yet. Come, my children."

While they followed Granny back to the living room in bewilderment, Nadeem murmured, "We'll figure it out later. She must not have noticed that weird sound."

Ava wasn't so sure. Secret laughter danced in Granny's eyes, and a playful expression lurked at one corner of her mouth.

Once again, Granny Buena settled herself in the middle of the sofa with Ava and Nadeem on either side of her. The cat curled into a doughnut shape on the handwoven multicolored rug at Ava's feet.

"Before we get started on the sewing," Granny said, "perhaps I should tell you the story of Ester ibn Evram the spice seller and Abdur Rahman the prince. Eh?"

Ava and Nadeem exclaimed "Yes!" at the same time—which immediately made Ava feel about four years old.

"All right, keridos. Cast your minds back in time, more than a thousand years. I shall take you to the city of Sabtah, at the northern tip of the African continent, in what is now the nation of Morocco."

Ava scooted closer to Granny, who put an arm around her.

"Ester ibn Evram is a smart and brave young Jewish girl. She and her mother, Sarai, are on their way to sell spices in the marketplace."

CHAPTER 3

"Hurry up, Ester!" Her mother, Sarai, called from the street outside their stone-and-mud house. "It's dawn already. We don't want to miss the early buyers. Quickly, my little one!"

Ester adjusted the scarf over her head with a sigh. Oh, how she hated being called "little"! She didn't need to be reminded that she was small for her age.

And it wasn't Ester's fault that she and her mother were running late. They had spent a whole hour taking care of Ester's older brother, Isaac: changing the wrappings on his injured ankle, setting food and water beside him, and arranging him comfortably for the long hours he would spend at home.

Now, Ester rushed to the little corner table in the downstairs room. On it were several sacks filled with herbs, roots, leaves, and seeds. Ester slung them over her thin shoulders. The sacks were big but not heavy.

By the time Ester joined her mother outside, Sarai was already pushing their handcart down the road. She'd packed it with spices , herbs, and oils. Her strides were strong and fast, and the cart's wooden wheels creaked as she hurried along.

Ester hastened after Sarai, holding up the hem of her robe and watching where she stepped. The dry dirt road from the Jewish Quarter to the market of Sabtah was dangerously uneven and pocked with craggy holes. It was here that Isaac had twisted his ankle on a loose stone the day before. In fact, this was why Ester was going with Sarai to the market this morning: to help sell in her brother's place. There was no one else to do it, since her father, Evram, was away in Spain on a buying trip.

Although Ester had visited the market many times to get supplies and food, she had never been allowed to sell at the family stall. This was her chance to prove herself. If she did well, perhaps her parents would let her continue doing the job.

Sarai said, "Your cousins Abigail and Nathan should arrive from Tangiers any day now. When they do, Nathan can take over at the stall. But until

21

then, I appreciate that you're willing to do your best to help, my dear."

Ester hardly remembered a single thing about her cousins Abigail and Nathan. She hadn't seen them since she was very small. But a strong dislike for them suddenly welled up in her heart. "I can sell spices by myself, Mother! You don't need my cousin."

Sarai smiled. "We'll see. If only you were taller, my dear! When people see you behind the table, they're bound to believe you're very young, and they'll try to cheat you."

So they were back to discussing her size again! Ester was too angry to say anything in reply.

"Come now, daughter—don't be upset," said Sarai. "You know that your cousins' visit has been arranged for a long while. Their parents want Nathan to learn more about the spice trade from us, and Abigail is hoping to get to know you better. The timing happens to be very fortunate, since Isaac is injured. Praise be to *Hashem*."

It would be no use to protest further. Ester simply sighed and kept walking while the sun rose higher over their heads. The pink and orange hues of the dawn sky faded into blue. Her leather-sandaled feet grew tired.

Her annoyance ebbed away, however, as they drew closer to the heart of the city. Near the main streets of Sabtah, nomads' tents clustered. Loud scraggly goats wandered around. Camels and gorgeous, well-kept horses stood patiently, tethered to wooden pegs in the ground. Women completely covered in black or brown garments moved among the beasts, carrying cooking pots and baskets.

Once they passed this colorful hubbub, Ester and Sarai entered the welcome shade of tall buildings, mud houses, and lean-tos in a hodgepodge of different styles. A confusion of noises and smells filled the air. Mules, carts, horses, and people pushed their way through the narrow streets.

Ester was taking everything in eagerly when a man approached her. He wore a white head wrap and a striped Berber robe. A large bird tethered to his arm lifted its red-tipped gray wings and squawked. "A talking parrot for you, little lady?" he asked with a smile.

There was that word—*little*—again.

"Stay close," Sarai warned. "No buying today. We're here to sell."

As if Ester would have asked for an expensive, bothersome parrot like a silly child! Though the bird *was* beautiful . . .

She shook her head at the man, who nodded politely and turned away.

Ester and Sarai rounded a corner. The street opened wide to reveal a brilliant turquoise bay lined with wooden docks.

Ahhh. The Mediterranean Sea.

Even this early, the sunlight bouncing off the water was bright enough to hurt Ester's eyes. But she savored the gleaming, shifting colors and wild, briny scent.

Here, on the northern tip of the African continent, Sabtah was only six miles of salt water away from Spain. Lovely Spain! Where oranges grew big and sweet, clear fountains flowed with cool water, and fragrant trees stretched their branches from lush courtyard gardens toward cloudless skies.

Imagining her father traveling through those enchanting lands made Ester's spirits as buoyant as the sea. She'd taken that journey with him several times. She hoped he would take her on the next trip.

"Pay attention, daughter." Sarai's sharp voice interrupted her daydreams. "It would be easy enough for someone to pull a sack from your shoulder and disappear into the crowd."

This was certainly true. Yet it was hard to keep an eye out for thieves when there was so much else to look at.

Like those tall sailing ships, for example, rocking in the harbor beside the many smaller fishing boats tied along the docks. They came from as far away as China and Russia. On their decks, sailors scurried to load and unload cargo. Seagulls cawed and swooped at the garbage the crews dumped over the ships' sides. Merchants wearing multicolored turbans haggled over bales, boxes, and clay jugs full of oil and grain.

The whole scene was alive with a glamorous air of adventure.

In this place, many kinds of people worked together, speaking Arabic as their common language. Although Ester's family spoke Hebrew at home, they were as proud of their fluent Arabic skills as they were of their strong network of relatives, friends, and business partners. Speaking multiple languages had helped them forge strong connections with Jews, Arabs, and Berbers alike.

"Sarai! Ester! Over here, dears!" a familiar voice rang out. Aunt Devora was waving to them from where she stood, behind a collapsible wooden table in the shade of a sand-colored building. Usually, Aunt Devora and Uncle Yosef walked to market with Ester's family. But today, they'd gone ahead while Sarai and Ester tended to Isaac.

As they drew near, Aunt Devora shouted, "Yosef got a good place in the shade and set up a stall for you. There—across the street from us."

Sarai approached her sister, calling out thanks. Ester followed. Aunt Devora's husband, Yosef, nodded at Ester fondly. Uncle Yosef was a silent fellow, but Ester liked him. He stood behind his wife, hands tucked into the sleeves of his robes. Though he had a serious face, his brown eyes always held a smile.

Uncle Yosef used the herbs Ester's father brought from Spain to mix medicines for sick animals. And unlike the services of a lot of other so-called animal healers, his cures really worked. This meant that his market stall was always surrounded by a bunch of bleating, neighing, unhappy beasts whose owners brought them for treatment.

After exchanging some chitchat with Sarai, Aunt Devora said, "Hello to you, Ester, little lovely! Are you ready to become a spice merchant now?" She reached out to pinch the girl's cheek.

Ester stepped backward to make pinching more difficult. "More than ready." She knew Aunt Devora was just teasing her.

But Ester was serious.

Ester's parents had been teaching her about herbs and spices since she was a tiny child. She knew the uses of sharp black pepper; fragrant lavender; hot, sweet red-brown cinnamon; savory bay leaf; and many, many more. She knew how to dry, hang, and grind them with a mortar and pestle. She could soak them in honey or olive oil to concoct cures for headaches, fevers, and sour stomachs. When she'd gone with her father on buying trips to Spain, Ester had met traders and farmers, and she'd learned where to find the huge markets where heaps of rich, brilliant spices were sold. She knew the prices to pay and the best ways to bargain. And she knew exactly how to help her mother prepare for a day of sales.

Sarai led the way across the street to the wooden table Uncle Yosef had assembled for them. While most sellers at the marketplace sat on blankets, Ester's family stood behind tables to make stealing more difficult. If someone snatched an item off a blanket, the thief would be gone by the time the seller scrambled to his feet. But if the seller was already standing up, a thief would have less of a head start. Spice sellers had to think of everything.

The first thing Sarai took out of the handcart was a copper weighing scale, which she placed in the middle of the table with great care. The scale had come from a faraway country and cost Ester's parents many coins. It was worth it, though, to be able to weigh their goods accurately so they could charge customers the right prices. This increased their reputation for fairness—and their popularity with customers.

"Watch me, Ester dear," Sarai said as her hands busily did their work. "Do you see how I put only small samples of the herbs on the table for smelling and tasting? The bulk of the spices must remain underneath, out of the sun and away from the air. This way, they stay fresh and keep their powers."

"I know that already, Mother."

"Oh, yes—bless you. Of course you do. Now, when someone wants to make a purchase, I will measure the herbs and spices on the scale. Then you can pack the items into the jars or sacks that people have brought with them while I collect the money or the goods we receive in exchange. If customers haven't brought their own container, you may use one of our cloth bags, but be sure to charge them for it."

Ester nodded. She knew all this too. She'd been overhearing her family's conversations about their business her whole life.

Soon enough, the first customers gathered in front of their table. Sarai took charge, recommending remedies and answering people's questions. Ester measured, packed, and handled payments—all the while watching for a chance to do more. Midway through the afternoon, a man with no beard approached the market stall. He wore a fancy, black-edged white tunic that looked Greek, though it was smudged and stained as if with much travel. Sarai was still giving cooking advice to a young woman who'd just bought some spices. While her mother was distracted, Ester gestured for the Greek man to come forward. Maybe he would be Ester's very first customer!

The man bowed slightly. *"As-salaamu alaykum.* Good morning to you, child. And to you, most honored lady." He inclined his head at Sarai.

Though his accent was Greek, his Arabic was perfect.

"Wa 'alaykum as-salaam," Ester replied in the same language, giving him the standard Arabic greeting.

"May I speak Hebrew with you?" he asked.

Ester started. This was unexpected—which made it suspicious.

Sarai frowned and turned her full attention to the Greek, while her previous customer departed with a bag of bay leaves and peppercorns. "You may speak to me, sir, not my daughter."

The Greek bowed again and said in Hebrew, "Honorable lady, many thanks. I have heard from the locals that you and your husband, Evram ibn Jacob, are very trustworthy."

"Thank you." Sarai sounded cautious.

The man bowed again. "I am Bedir, servant to a most upright master. He is looking for someone to take him across the sea to Spain. But he wishes to do it privately. Might you or your husband be able to find someone among the Jews to take us across?"

"Why do you ask this of a spice seller?" Sarai wrapped the edge of her scarf more tightly around her head as if to protect herself from something more than dust and the hot sun. "There are many boats on the harbor with owners who make a living ferrying people across the sea. You are free to hire one."

Bedir picked up a small corked bottle of lavender oil, which many customers used to heal cuts and help with sleep. He pretended to inspect it as he continued speaking in a voice so low that Ester could barely hear it. "My noble master doesn't wish to hire one of the regular channel boats. He would rather travel more . . . discreetly. Your family is known for their long-distance trade, so you can cross the sea from here to Jabal Tāriq at any time, without anyone finding it strange. If you keep this a secret from our enemies, my master will pay you very well."

This was strange and worrying. Ester felt a coldness clutch her insides. She looked up at her mother.

Sarai stood straight and proud, her eyes flashing. Yet she, too, spoke in a low murmur. "You talk of enemies, yet we know nothing of who you are—and nothing of your intentions. Who are these enemies you speak of? I can tell by your accent and your mode of dress that you are not Muslim, nor are you a Jew, though you speak Hebrew. I warn you, if you plan to do harm to anyone in this community, I will do my utmost to stop you."

The man replied in a desperate whisper. "My master poses no threat to anyone in this town—Muslim, Jew, Christian, or any other believer or unbeliever. Our enemies have pursued us here from . . . elsewhere. They are not the people of Sabtah."

Ester could tell from her mother's grave face that she was not convinced.

Bedir's tone became pleading. "My master is young, brave, and alone—except for me." The stranger glanced cautiously around. "I beg of you, please help us. His life is in danger. He is being pursued by a band of men for political reasons, and they have sympathizers lurking everywhere."

Ester trembled. She knew she should say nothing. Yet the question came from her mouth before she could stop it: "Who is your master?"

Sarai placed a warning hand on Ester's shoulder.

But Bedir nodded. "Very well. If I am asking your help, you have the right to know. My master has many names and titles. But you would know him as Abdur Rahman, Prince of the Umayyads."

Ester's knees wobbled. For a second, she actually felt as if she might faint.

The Umayyads were Muslim royalty who lived in far-off Syria and had ruled over many lands. A short time ago, their dynasty had been overthrown by a different family, the Abbasids, who now ruled in their place.

"But none of the Umayyads survived," Sarai whispered.

"That is not true, worthy lady," the man said. "My noble master escaped, with my help. We faced many evils in order to arrive here alive. My master is the only Umayyad prince left, and we must get him to his family's friends in Spain, where he will be safe."

Sarai drew in a deep breath of shock. Ester knew she must be thinking of how dangerous it was for common folk to become involved in the rivalries of caliphs and princes. Then Sarai suddenly raised her voice, as if she was trying hard to sound casual. "That will be three silver coins for the bottle of skin oil, please. And, Ester, make up a bag of fever bark below the table for this gentleman."

Ester was grateful for the excuse to drop to the ground and hide under the stall. She wouldn't have been able to keep her face neutral much longer, and her troubled expression might have attracted unwanted attention.

What Bedir was asking would be a risk, yes, but the trip from Sabtah to Jabal Tāriq was short. In fact, the big rocky outcropping of Sabtah and the rock of Jabal Tāriq were so close to each other that they were known as "the brothers." Ester had made the passage with her father many times. She'd even steered their boat for stretches of the journey while he rested. This mission was doable—and if it could save someone's life, surely it was worthwhile.

She heard her mother whisper to Bedir, "I make no promises. Yet I am a Jew, and my people do not stand back when the life of any person is in danger. I will speak with my family and see what we can do."

"Thank you!" Bedir breathed.

"Come back to our stall here in the marketplace tomorrow, and I will tell you what has been decided."

Ester's heart beat so hard that she felt it in her throat.

"My lady," the Greek said, "your heart is generous. I will be here tomorrow. Meanwhile, take this. If I somehow become separated from the prince, it will be a sign to him that the person wearing it is a representative of your family, whom he can trust. It is also a pledge. If you keep faith with us, we will reward you well."

Ester peeked over the stall. The man held out a silver object set with tiny red rubies that gleamed in the sunlight.

It was a button.

CHAPTER 4

"Wait!" said Ava. "Are you saying that the silver button Bedir gave to Ester is the same one you showed us from the Button Box?"

Granny nodded.

Nadeem's mouth fell open. "No way!" he exclaimed. "Abdur Rahman owned that actual button?"

When Granny nodded again, he added, "It must be worth a fortune!"

"Oh, my child, we would never sell it," she replied. "How could we? *Vender el sol por comprar kandelas?*"

"*Would we sell the sun to buy candles?*" Ava translated. Granny had been teaching her Ladino since she was very little, and she was pretty good at it by now. Meanwhile, Nadeem had been learning Arabic.

"However," Granny said, "I must admit we have no actual proof that the prince ever owned the button. We only have our family wisdom, handed down through the ages."

Ava put a hand on Granny's arm. "What about the rest of the story? Don't leave us hanging."

Granny's face took on a mischievous air. "You'll find out the rest soon. But come now, darlings—we need to sew the button back onto Ava's shirt. I've been so caught up in my storytelling that we haven't even started on it yet."

Why was Granny Buena obsessing about sewing? Ava thought she might pop out of her skin with impatience.

Granny handed a slim silver needle to Nadeem, along with a strand of white thread. "Can you thread the needle, beloved?"

"Uh, sure, I guess," said Nadeem. "How hard could it be? Bismillah." Nadeem tried to insert the end of of the thread into the narrow opening, his fingers fumbling.

Ava thought she could do it better. She loved crafting things like friendship bracelets and was pretty good with her hands. But she kept quiet. She could just imagine *that* conversation!

While Nadeem kept trying, Granny said, "Keridos, sewing is a lot like life. You are the needle that stands strong, while life flows through you like thread. You must guide your life, the way the needle guides the thread, to make strong, beautiful things. Like a needle, you have the power to mend what is torn. Watch for the opportunity to fix what has gone wrong in the world, my children. You never know when it might come up, and you must be ready for it."

Nadeem interrupted, exclaiming, "Granny, this is impossible! The hole's too small."

"Try pushing the needle over the thread, not pushing the thread into the needle," Granny suggested.

With this new trick, he got it on the first try. "Whoa!"

Ava laughed. "Go, Nadeem!"

"We old people are good for some things, eh?" Granny remarked. "When you're stuck, dears, always try a different way." She tightened a loop at the long end of Nadeem's thread. "This knot is like an anchor. It holds the thread and the button in place. Everything in life needs an anchor. Show me where the button should go, Ava, my dear."

"Okay." Ava rested her arm on her grandmother's knee and offered up the place where the button had been torn away. Granny made quick work of finishing up the sewing and clipped the thread with a tiny gold scissors.

"As you see, it needed a few more passes with the needle to make the button stay," Granny said.

"Is there some kind of important life lesson in that too?" Nadeem asked.

Ava knew he was joking, but apparently Granny didn't.

"Oh, yes. There is always work to be done, even after you think you've reached your goal." She got up from the sofa and stretched her back. "*La, la, la,* my children. I'm tired after all the baking I did today. And my folk dancing class at the community center this morning was very vigorous. I need an afternoon nap." She hid a tiny yawn behind her hand.

Nadeem looked disappointed. "But, Granny, what about the story you were telling us?"

"I'm afraid we'll have to leave the rest of Ester ibn Evram's adventure for later. Feel free to get started on your homework in the dining room, but please make sure not to damage the Button Box while you're there."

Nadeem looked at Ava.

Ava looked at Nadeem.

Time to solve the mystery of the humming button.

"Sure, Granny." Ava got up and hugged her. "Have a good sleep."

"Just a second, Granny Buena," Nadeem said. "Before you go . . . do you know what that writing on the side of the Button Box says? It looks a lot like Arabic to me—but not exactly."

"Smart boy! It's Kufic, the earliest written form of Arabic," she replied. "That inscription always makes me think of the Jewish idea of *tikkun olam*. Many of us believe we have the divinely given task to repair what has gone wrong in the world. This is what the writing on the Button Box says:

> *"Mend hearts,*
> *and fasten together*
> *the fabric of time."*

CHAPTER 5

With Granny upstairs, the cousins hovered over the Button Box at the dining room table, sharing a sense of awe and excitement.

Though Ava felt there might be something dangerous about ancient buttons that made eerie sounds, she told herself not to be silly and removed the heavy lid. Then she carefully scooped out a handful of buttons, looking for Ester's pin.

Nadeem grabbed some too, and spread out his batch on the table. "Ooh, look at this one. It has a face painted on it! I wonder who this was."

When she turned to look at the tiny painted portrait Nadeem was holding, Ava caught sight of something else: a unique silver-and-ruby sparkle. "Found it!" She lifted the glittering pin. Nadeem put down the other button and leaned in for a closer look.

"Yes! It's the button of Ester ibn Evram!" His voice was eager. "Now we can figure out what the humming noise was."

"Right!" Ava exclaimed. "Let's do an experiment. The noise happened when we touched the button together. Why don't we try touching it again?"

Nadeem put a fingertip to the button in Ava's hand. A faint, whispery musical sound rose into the air between them.

Ava jumped. The button slipped from her grasp and landed on the table with a small thump.

The sound stopped.

"Okay. Wow. This is really weird," Nadeem said in a slightly shaky voice.

"But is it weird in a cool, exciting way or weird in a 'the two kids had no idea that a dangerous power lurked inside the button, waiting for a chance to destroy them' kind of way?" Ava asked.

"I don't know."

"What should we do?"

Right then, Sheba hopped onto the table. The opal hanging from her collar, which had been shiny before, now glowed a fiery orange.

Ava stared first at the jewel, then into the cat's

hypnotic hazel eyes. A bizarre thought popped into her head, seemingly from out of nowhere. Something about . . . sewing the special Ester ibn Evram button onto her school sweatshirt.

Wait. What kind of idea was that?

A gorgeous piece of silver and ruby jewelry would look ultra-dorky on a sweatshirt! Especially one that said *Canyon School Cardinals* on it. Besides, Granny would never let her leave the house wearing such a precious family possession.

While Ava was busy objecting to her own idea (it *was* her idea, wasn't it?), the opal on Sheba's collar blazed even more brightly. Gazing into its shifting, multicolored depths, Ava felt peculiar. She found herself saying, "Hey, Nadeem, don't you think this button would look cool on my school sweatshirt?"

"Yeah!" Nadeem flashed her a thumbs-up. That was weird too. Why wasn't he telling her how silly the suggestion was?

Still, Ava hopped up and retrieved the sweatshirt from her backpack in the front entryway.

When she returned, Nadeem had already snagged Granny's needle and thread from the coffee table. Ava tossed him the sweatshirt. He began sewing the button onto the crewneck collar, exactly the way Granny had taught them.

While Nadeem worked, Sheba placed a paw on the cushion beside him, as if in support of his efforts. Nadeem glanced at the cat in surprise. "Do you think Sheba smells the honey cake I just ate? She's never been this friendly to me before."

"Well, maybe *you've* never been friendly to *her* before."

"Clearly she's impressed with my sewing talent. There—done!" Nadeem lifted the sweatshirt proudly. "I should open a tailoring shop."

Ava stood and put out a hand. "Here. Let me try it on."

As soon as she pulled the sweatshirt over her head, the floor shifted beneath her feet. She lost her balance. "Aaaack!"

"Earthquake!" Nadeem shouted.

The odd, many-voiced humming sound started again, louder than before. Darkness descended on them like an inky cloud. Nadeem clutched Ava's arm for balance.

Then the rocking stopped as suddenly as it had begun. The darkness faded.

"Where are we?" Nadeem's voice sounded as scared as Ava felt.

She looked around. They were standing by a turquoise sea, near a busy dock, in blinding hot sunshine.

Wherever this was, it sure wasn't Granny's living room.

CHAPTER 6

Nadeem let go of Ava's arm, and the humming stopped.

The two of them turned around and around in the middle of the dusty street, gaping at passersby who wore loose robes and either head scarves or wrapped turbans. On one side of them, the road dropped away to reveal an incredibly blue ocean harbor. Weather-beaten ships tied up along a wharf rocked slightly in the twinkling, choppy sea. Sailors moved purposefully across the decks of the ships, carrying crates and strangely shaped clay bottles.

Along the other side of the street, people sat or squatted on the ground with a dizzying rainbow of goods spread out on cloths in front of them. Ava glimpsed bright-red tomatoes, green and yellow and orange peppers, pinkish clay pots, blue and purple woven rugs, bundles of twigs with shiny green leaves that perfumed the air with a minty smell, and much more.

Why does everything seem so strangely familiar? Ava wondered. As if she'd seen it all in a dream.

Nadeem said, "Are you thinking what I'm thinking?"

She made a face. "I'm thinking I've lost my marbles."

"I'm thinking this place looks a whole lot like the city in the story Granny Buena was telling us."

That was it—the reason this place looked familiar! "No way," she breathed. "Impossible!"

"It can't be impossible if it just happened."

Ava had to admit that she couldn't think of any other explanation. It really seemed like, somehow, she and Nadeem had landed in the ancient past.

"Hey!" Nadeem jumped backward as a cart with big wooden wheels scraped by him.

Her attention drawn back to her cousin, Ava gasped. "Nadeem! Look at you! Look at *us*!"

He held out his arms. He was dressed in the same type of brown robes that the people around them wore. He lifted first one foot, then the other, to stare at the leather sandals that had appeared on them.

Ava wore a similar outfit. She reached up to touch the woven headscarf that covered her brown curls.

A grin inched across Nadeem's face. "Sweet! Ava, this is an adventure! *Subhan Allah!*"

"Seriously, Nadeem?" She stared at him. "This is a *problem*. We could be stuck here in Sabtah forever—if this is really Sabtah."

"But it was our family button that brought us here. I mean, Granny never would've shown us the buttons if they were going to put us in danger. I'm sure we'll be fine."

Ava *wasn't* so sure. Their own time and place could feel scary enough sometimes. An unfamiliar city in the distant past probably posed even more threats. She sincerely hoped they wouldn't be around long enough to find out.

Before she could explain this to Nadeem, a light scratch on her leg and a tiny *meow* distracted her.

No way. "Sheba! What in the world are you doing here?" Ava bent to pick up the cat from the unpaved street.

"Wow!" Nadeem exclaimed. "If Sheba's here, maybe Granny Buena is too!"

Now there was a nice idea. Holding Sheba tight,

Ava stood on the tips of her toes to scan the crowd. A lady who was definitely not Granny bumped into her and let out an annoyed grunt. She was carrying a clay jar on her head, and she adjusted it before walking on.

Ava's hope fizzled.

Sheba nuzzled Ava's face in a comforting way, more like a dog than a cat. Then a little man selling blankets nearby tossed her a suspicious frown.

"What's with him?" Ava nodded in the blanket seller's direction.

"Maybe he thinks we want to shoplift a blanket."

Nadeem was kidding, but Ava felt a flicker of alarm. If she and Nadeem got into trouble here, they'd be toast. How would they deal with the police—or whatever law enforcement looked like here—when they couldn't even speak the language? It was Arabic, right? And Ester ibn Evram spoke Hebrew too. Ava suddenly regretted that she didn't go to Hebrew school with her friends Rochelle and Eliza. She made a mental note to ask Mom about signing up as soon as she got back to her rightful time and place . . . if she ever did get back. She felt a sudden pang, missing her mom as if she hadn't seen her for weeks. "We'd better keep moving. We don't want to attract attention."

As they hurried away from the frowning blanket guy, Nadeem said, "Ester ibn Evram's button brought us here. There's got to be a reason—something we're supposed to do."

Ava shook her head. "I don't like this at all. Let's touch the button together, quick. If it brought us to the past, it should be able to take us back to our time. And Sheba too."

He sighed. "Okay. But I still think we could have an awesome adventure if we stayed." He looked over at her. His eyes widened with shock. "Ava, the button was on your sweatshirt—and your sweatshirt is gone!" He waved at the drapey garments that had replaced her school clothes.

Heart pounding, Ava dropped Sheba and frantically searched her wool robe, then felt up and down the simple linen dress underneath. When her fingers found the special family button pinned to the inner dress, she threw a grateful look up to heaven. "Oh, thank you!" She pushed the folds of wool aside and bent toward Nadeem. "Let's go."

Nadeem pressed the glittering pin like it was part of a game console. So did Ava. They held their breath.

The air didn't sparkle. The earth didn't shift. And there was no hum at all.

They pushed again.

"Well," Nadeem said, after an awful minute that felt like an hour to Ava, "I guess this can mean one of two things. Either 'welcome to our new home in the past' . . . or, like I said before, we've got a mission—some kind of special job to do. We can't go home till it's done."

Sheba gazed up at them and meowed. Almost as if she were backing up what Nadeem had said.

"Then I guess we'd better find out what our mission is," Ava sighed.

"But how?"

Just then, the voice of a woman across the street floated over to them in a language that definitely wasn't English. Ava realized with amazement that she could understand every word.

"Ester! Ester ibn Evram, where are you?" the lady shouted. "Why aren't you helping your mother?"

A petite, dark-haired girl popped up from underneath a stall table at the nearest corner. She held up a small sack. "I'm here, Aunt Devora! Just getting some fever bark!" Her voice sounded wobbly, as if she was uncomfortable with what she was saying . . . or even as if she were lying.

"That's Ester from Granny's story!" Ava gasped.

"And do you see the man in front of her stall—the one in the white tunic?"

"Bedir the Greek!" Nadeem cried. "So the lady next to Ester must be her mom, Sarai."

"Wow," Ava breathed. "I think we got here at the exact same time and place where Granny's story left off! What if we're here to help finish the story? To help Prince Abdur Rahman escape?"

"I wish we'd heard the rest of it. Then we'd know what comes next."

Ava frowned down at Sheba, as if somehow the cat could tell her. She remembered what Granny Buena had said about life being like a thread and people being like needles. *You must guide your life, the way the needle guides the thread.* "Maybe what comes next is whatever we decide," said Ava.

Sheba made a small yowly sound and bounded across the street. That seemed like a clear hint.

Ava squared her shoulders and headed toward the stall. She wasn't sure what she would do or say once she was face to face with her ancestors, but she figured she'd cross that bridge when she came to it.

"I'm right behind you," Nadeem said.

Their approach attracted Sarai's attention. She looked past Bedir the Greek and met Ava's gaze. Her expression changed from worry over whatever Bedir had been telling her to . . . recognition.

She recognized Ava and Nadeem? Not possible.

"Abigail! Nathan!" Sarai exclaimed.

Ava clapped a hand on her chest and made a "Me?" face.

Ester's mother nodded and kept beckoning. "Yes, my children—you've found the right place. It's been a long while since we've seen you. I'm your Aunt Sarai!"

Nadeem whispered, "She thinks we're her niece and nephew. Should we tell her we're not them?"

"No. Go with it." Ava put on a big smile and led the way over to the stall. "Hello, Aunt Sarai!" Then she clapped her hand over her mouth to stifle a shriek of surprise. She'd spoken another language!

Nadeem gaped at her. "That was Arabic!"

"And very good Arabic it is." Sarai patted Ava's shoulder. "Your parents have taught you well, Abigail."

Bedir the Greek stood by, watching. His broad face was smooth and expressionless. But Ava figured he was pretty annoyed that two kids had interrupted his important assignment for Prince Abdur Rahman.

Sarai planted a big kiss on Ava's cheeks—first

one, then the other. "We are so happy to have you, my dears!"

From across the road, the lady who'd called to Ester earlier shouted, "Is that darling Abigail and Nathan?" It was Aunt Devora, from Granny's story.

Aunt Devora hurried over, pushing her way past a pair of sick goats that Uncle Yosef was treating with herbs. Her headscarf fell back from a super-twisty mop of black and gray hair. "Oh, children, how beautiful you are! How grown up! Look at that face." She pinched Nadeem's chin while her big arm bangles bopped his nose. "I'd recognize you anywhere, Nathan! You're exactly like your father, Baruch! How is his surgery business going? Does he need more medicines? Sarai can provide them! Oh, how much you look like Baruch!"

Nadeem rubbed his nose.

Sarai's eyes twinkled. "Our nephew does indeed resemble our brother."

Ava started to relax a bit. This scene reminded her of the fuss their out-of-town relatives made over her at Granny's huge Passover seders. Though these women were strangers to her, somehow they also felt like family.

Which, of course, they were.

Bedir the Greek was still standing beside them in silence. Ava realized he must be waiting for an answer to a very important question. A question of life and death.

Sarai seemed to suddenly remember he was there. She moved aside to speak to Bedir in an undertone. "Come back to our stall here in the marketplace tomorrow, and I will tell you what has been decided."

Bedir nodded and said something to Sarai in a voice too low for Ava to distinguish the words. He handed her something, and Sarai gave him a corked bottle of oil.

With a bow, Bedir tucked the bottle inside his robe and disappeared into the marketplace crowd.

Sarai watched him go, worry in her face.

Meanwhile, Aunt Devora hugged Nadeem. "Isn't this boy precious?"

Uncle Yosef showed up, apparently finished with the goats. Nadeem quickly hopped behind Ava as if to fend off another crushing hug. But Yosef's greeting was more reserved than his wife's had been. He simply clasped Ava's and Nadeem's shoulders in a friendly way, then glanced off to one side. "Aren't you eager to greet your cousins, little Ester?"

Turning to face Ester ibn Evram, Ava felt suddenly

shy. Her ancestor was indeed quite petite, making it obvious why everyone kept calling her "little." But what Ava really noticed about Ester were large amber eyes, brown skin, and curly dark hair covered with a dove-gray scarf.

"Ester dear," Aunt Devora gushed, "now that Abigail and Nathan have arrived, you don't need to help your mother sell in the marketplace after all! Isn't that convenient?"

Ester's cool glance made it clear that she didn't think it was convenient at all.

"Greetings, Cousin Ester." Nadeem made a respectful gesture that included placing his hand on his chest. Ava knew it was a polite Arab custom.

She caught her breath. Would the family now realize that Nadeem wasn't actually who they'd thought he was?

Apparently not. Ester returned Nadeem's gesture, while Aunt Devora peppered him and Ava with so many questions that the kids didn't even have to pretend to know the answers: "How is your mother? How is your father? How are things with the community in Tangiers?"

While her aunt chattered, Ester stared at Ava and Nadeem without a hint of welcome. Considering that their visit was derailing Ester's plans to prove herself as a spice seller, Ava understood how her ancestor must feel.

Suddenly a small, sleek feline form leaped to the top of the spice table—and from the table into Ester's arms.

Ester and Ava both cried out at the same time: "Sheba!"

Huh? How did Ester know Granny Buena's pet cat?

Nadeem shot Ava a warning look. Ava quickly schooled her face into what she hoped was a calm and collected expression, feeling grateful that Ester didn't seem to have noticed her blunder.

"Cousins, this is our beloved little companion, Sheba," Ester said, stroking the cat's head. "She must have followed us when we left home today."

Her mother reached over to pet Sheba too. "I wouldn't have believed it possible for her to walk so far on her own."

"Amazing that a cat could come so far," Ava agreed, with a meaningful look at Nadeem.

Nadeem quoted Granny Buena with a grin. "I guess in this family, many things are possible that might seem impossible at first."

"That's true, Nathan," Ester said, speaking directly to him for the first time. "But making unlikely things possible usually takes a lot of courage."

He smiled. "I guess Sheba's one brave cat."

Ava hoped she could be brave too. She had a feeling that while she was in Sabtah, she was going to need all the courage she could get.

CHAPTER 7

A cluster of buyers had gathered at the spice stall while the family had been welcoming Ava and Nadeem.

"We'd better attend to our customers," said Sarai. "Nathan, we appreciate you being willing to take over."

Ava spoke without thinking. "But, Aunt Sarai, can't Cousin Ester do it?" When Sarai frowned at her, she stammered, "Um . . . I mean . . . Nathan has never sold at a stall like this before. Maybe he should learn more gradually, and Ester can be his teacher." She hoped she sounded respectful.

Ester gave Ava a surprised, grateful look. "Mother, she's right. Cousin Nathan doesn't know how our family business works yet. Maybe I could be the one to explain it to him."

Sarai shook her head. "I can do the explaining,

daughter. Now take Cousin Abigail for a nice walk around Sabtah. She will want see the sights."

Ester sighed and turned to Ava. "They don't want us here. We're not *boys*."

Well, this was awkward.

But there was no way Ava was going to let herself get separated from Nadeem. "Um, Aunt Sarai? Could I stay around for a while and watch you and Nathan work? Just for today. I'm curious to see how you do business. Maybe Ester can show both me and my brother around later."

Nadeem gave her a thumbs-up from inside the sleeve of his robe.

Sarai's absent expression turned into a warm smile. "I can tell you are a clever and industrious girl, Abigail. Of course, if you really want to, you may sit by that wall over there and see how it's done. If you grow bored, feel free to wander the marketplace with Ester, as long as you stay together and are cautious."

Once the two of them were sitting by the wall, with Sheba cuddled up in Ava's lap, Ester bent close to Ava and whispered, "Cousin, it was kind of you to suggest that I could help sell. I was very much hoping to take my brother's place at the stall today."

Ava frowned. "I'm sorry, Ester. We didn't mean to mess things up for you."

"It's not your fault," Ester said with a sigh. "What I want is something I'm not likely to get, but that doesn't mean I won't keep fighting for it. Now, enough about me. I want to be a good host while you're here, and I hope you'll tell me if there's anything you'd like to see or do. How long are you staying?"

"Oh . . . I'm not really sure. It depends, I think."

If Nadeem was right about them having a mission to accomplish, and if that mission involved Prince Abdur Rahman, Ava had no idea how long the task would take to complete. She couldn't help wondering why the Button Box would have chosen a couple of kids like her and Nadeem to do the job. Could it be that the two of them had some kind of crucial knowledge from the future that would make the whole escape safe and easy?

Probably not.

She and Nadeem weren't diplomats who could negotiate with the prince's enemies or tech geniuses who could build a special vehicle to speed the prince on his way. In fact, she had to admit that they didn't really know how to do much except write five-paragraph essays, take tests, and play games. Ava decided that if she ever got home, she would acquire some useful skills, like . . . like . . . lighting a fire without matches, or . . . self-defense, or something. Maybe she could take those classes right after she finished with Hebrew school. It was exhausting even to think about.

For the next hour, Ava and Ester watched as Sarai sold remedy after remedy, with Nadeem helping her weigh the items on the scale. One young mother wanted an animal bone soaked in a licorice-flavored herb to help her teething baby. An old man needed a mixture of honey, mint, and wormwood to rub into his aching knees and knuckles. A man who had cut his hand needed it packed in seaweed that had first been dipped in lavender, eucalyptys, and olive oil to disinfect it.

Finally, the sun began to wane and the market-place started to empty out.

"My, my!" Sarai declared, wiping her hands on the front of her robe. "What a busy day. Before any more people come to buy from us, we should take Nathan and Abigail home to get some rest. Ester, my little daughter, why don't you go buy some fish for dinner while I break down the stall? And get twice as much as usual, dear, because we have more mouths to feed!"

Ava suspected that Sarai was eager to get home so she could talk to her relatives about saving—or not saving—Prince Abdur Rahman's life.

"Can we help you pack up, Aunt Sarai?" Nadeem offered, gesturing at himself and Ava.

"Yes, dear boy," Sarai gave him a distracted smile. "Bless you."

As Ava and Nadeem gathered up spices to put back into Ester's sacks, Ava whispered to Nadeem, "Be careful, okay? The more time we spend here, the more chances there are to make mistakes. We don't want people to get suspicious. Don't offer up too much information."

He nodded. "And let's hope they don't ask for any!"

When Ester returned with a fishy-smelling bundle, her mother Sarai crossed the street to say goodbye to Aunt Devora and Uncle Yosef, who were still busy helping customers with unhappy animals. Then with a smile and a "Come along, children," Sarai led Ester, Ava, and Nadeem down the unpaved road.

Nadeem pushed the cart for Sarai—an honor that he pretended to be happy about, which made

Ava want to giggle. Sheba rode on top of the cart. Ava herself was carrying the almost-weightless fragrant spice sacks, while Ester had tucked her dinner purchase into a sling of cloth at her hip.

They headed toward the base of a big green-and-brown hill in the distance. As they left behind the more crowded part of Sabtah, the road brought them to higher ground, giving them a better view of the surrounding area. Ava exclaimed: "Oh! The sea is on both sides of us!"

"Yes, cousin," Ester said with a little smile. "This is a peninsula."

"The water's so incredibly blue." Nadeem paused and pointed. "What's that big shape on the horizon over there, across the sea?"

"Jabal Tāriq," Aunt Sarai replied. "The great rock that marks the entrance to Spain. There is a prosperous trading port at its base. It's said you can buy anything there, anything at all. Silk and jewels from the east. Brilliant feathers from the far south. And, of course, every kind of spice."

"That's why my father makes the trip there so often," added Ester. "Many ships carrying the rarer spices skip right over Sabtah and go straight to Jabal Tāriq."

"It sounds exciting," Ava said. "I'd love to see it."

Ester said, "You would indeed love it. But if you're here when my father makes his next trip, he will probably take your brother there instead of you. Because you're a girl." The slightly bitter note in her voice was hard to miss. And who could blame her?

Ava lay a hand on Ester's arm. Ester placed her own hand on top of Ava's for a second.

Nadeem glanced in another direction and exclaimed again. "And just look at that river! I've never seen a river so sparkly and clean in my whole life!"

The girls drew apart, and Ester gave Nadeem a quizzical look. "Is the water very dirty where you come from, cousin?"

A slightly panicked expression flickered across Nadeem's face. Ava realized that Nadeem had been comparing the clear Sabtah river to polluted rivers in the future.

Sheba gave a meow, jumped from the cart to Nadeem's shoulder, and nuzzled his neck as if to reassure him. He petted the cat and said carefully, "What I meant to say was that it's the most beautiful river I've ever seen, that's all. You're lucky to live here."

Sarai nodded. "Indeed, my nephew. We thank Hashem for the blessing of this beautiful and welcoming town. It would take a great deal to convince me to leave a place such as this."

Sarai didn't sound suspicious. Ava drew in a deep breath of relief—which turned into an astonished gasp. The air was so sweet! Out here, away from the busy heart of the city, the slight breeze was outrageously fresh. She could smell the sea . . . and some kind of plant . . . the dry earth . . . even a pure watery scent rising from the banks of the river, where birds had gathered in groups so big, they must be fishing for something. *Or,* she wondered, *were there just more birds in the past?*

What a difference a thousand years could make!

Nadeem's wide-eyed gaze met hers, and she was sure he was thinking along the same lines.

Sheba hopped back onto the cart, and the little group began walking again. Sarai started to sing an upbeat little song in Hebrew, and Ava's spirits lifted.

Ester turned her attention back to Nadeem. "I hope you don't mind my asking, but why does your father wish you to learn the merchant trade? I would have thought he would be training you in his own business instead."

Uh-oh. Ava couldn't remember what it was their "father," Baruch, did for a living back in Tangiers, although she knew Aunt Devora had mentioned it.

"Uh . . ." Nadeem flushed. "The thing is, I'm not really very good at, um, doing surgery. I get sick when I see blood, and I honestly don't have the patience for it."

Surgery! Yes, that was Baruch's job. What a relief that Nadeem had remembered! And he'd managed to avoid actually telling any lies.

Ester looked at Nadeem with a thoughtful expression.

Hoping to distract Ester and lighten the mood, Ava joked, "Speak for yourself, brother. I personally would love to sew together a bunch of gruesome wounds."

Ester gave her a curious but not unsympathetic look. "Then it's a shame that girls don't become surgeons. Maybe someday you will find a way to follow your dream."

Ava grimaced. *Argh. Why did I bring attention to myself?* Instead of protesting that she had just been kidding, she simply agreed. "Yes. Maybe."

"Hush, my daughter," said Sarai to Ester. "The discerning among us recognize that the greatest good comes from doing our best with the specific tasks Hashem has set before us, rather than yearning after tasks which belong to others."

"All the tasks set before us, or just some of them?" Ester gave her mother a very direct look. "Even the unexpected ones, which might be dangerous?"

Sarai actually paled.

Ava knew what they both were thinking of.

Then Nadeem casually dropped a verbal bombshell. "Hey, have either of you heard the rumor that Prince Abdur Rahman was seen in Sabtah this week?"

Sarai looked shocked. "Where did you hear such a thing?"

Ava winced. "And why would you bring it up right now, *darling brother*?"

He shrugged innocently. "I heard something about it before we got to your market stall today."

Ava had to hand it to him: technically, this was true.

Nadeem continued, "Just now, Aunt Sarai, you mentioned the tasks before us. I wonder whether we should, I don't know . . . try to find the prince and help him, maybe? It could be that the Most High wants us to."

Ester's big amber eyes got even bigger. She glanced at her mother. "Perhaps you're right, Cousin Nathan. If that task came before me, I would hope to have the courage to save the prince's life."

Aunt Sarai started walking faster, as if she meant to leave them behind. Ester stepped up her pace, drawing ahead far enough so that when the two began to argue, Ava couldn't hear their words.

"Seems like that didn't go over very well," Nadeem said to Ava.

"Well, everything happening with Prince Abdur Rahman is supposed to be a big secret," said Ava. "And you just brought him up like it was no big deal. What kind of reaction were you expecting?"

"I was hoping to kind of nudge Sarai in the right direction," said Nadeem. "She seems on the fence about helping Abdur Rahman. I mean, isn't that what we're here for—to make sure he escapes Sabtah?"

"That's our theory. But we can't be sure."

"Getting the prince to Spain is a great thing, whether it's our mission or not. So, *Insh'Allah*, let's hope Sarai takes what I said as a sign and makes the right choice."

"Good point," Ava admitted. "That was a whole lot of quick thinking, Nadeem. I'm impressed."

Just then, a faint call to afternoon prayer rose from the mosque in the town behind them.

"Time for some more quick thinking," said Nadeem. "Can you push the cart while I go pray?"

Ava glanced at Ester and Sarai up ahead. "What if they notice you're gone?"

"Say I'm getting a closer look at the river. Which will be true!"

"Okay, go for it. I'll slow down so you can catch up when you're finished."

Nadeem disappeared behind a stand of trees. Ava slowed to a snail's pace. Luckily, Ester and Sarai were too caught up in their argument to even look over their shoulders.

When Nadeem reappeared alongside her, she sighed with relief. "That felt like forever," she breathed.

He laughed and took hold of the cart's handles again. "I was only gone for a few minutes. But I made them count."

Ava was glad.

Because asking for divine help right now actually seemed like a very good idea.

CHAPTER 8

It seemed like forever before Sarai finally announced, "Here we are! The Jewish Quarter!"

Hot and thirsty and hoping for comfort at journey's end, Ava felt disappointment lodge like a hard little stone in her throat. She'd imagined fancy domes, black metal hanging lanterns casting complicated shadows, and beautiful colored tiles on the walls, like she'd seen in pictures of old Jerusalem.

But the Jewish Quarter was a collection of about thirty small, simple dwellings made of clay. Ava spotted one building that had to be a synagogue because a Star of David was sculpted above its door. It had a smaller enclosed space attached to it—probably a *mikvah*, where people could take ritual baths.

There were animal pens or chicken coops next

to some of the houses. Sounds of hens clucking and the strangely human-like braying of goats greeted the travelers as they stumbled forward on aching feet.

Ava wished the miraculous power of the Button Box could have somehow let her and Nadeem keep their sneakers.

Sarai led them to one of the little houses. Sheba sprang off the cart and vanished into the shadows. "Nathan, you may leave the cart by the entrance here," said Sarai. "Little Ester, go fetch water, please."

Wow, Sarai kept doubling down on that "little" stuff, Ava reflected. No wonder it was constantly on Ester's mind.

Ester picked up a large clay jar that stood on the doorstep, swung it onto her head with a practiced flair, and moved away. Meanwhile, Sarai removed her sandals and placed them on the step, so the kids did too. And when Sarai reached out to touch the mezuzah on the wall outside the door, then brought her fingers reverently to her lips, Ava copied her actions.

As soon as they stepped into the cool darkness of the house, a voice from the far corner of the room called, "Shalom, Mother! Who's this you've brought with you?"

Ava peered toward the corner, her eyes adjusting to the dimness. She made out the shape of a lanky older boy lying among some blankets on the clean, dry, packed clay floor. There was a basin of water, an empty plate with the remains of a meal on it, and a simple clay cup beside him. This had to be Isaac, Ester's brother.

"Shalom, my beautiful son!" Sarai crossed the room and pushed open a rough wooden shutter—just a crack, to let in some light but keep out the heat. Now Ava could see a handwoven red and orange rug in the center of the floor. A clay lamp hung from the ceiling, along with upside-down flowers and what looked like grasses. Hanging up grass was a strange way to decorate, Ava thought. Putting the plants in a vase would be a whole lot easier.

Nadeem followed her gaze and said, "They're drying out herbs. You know, lavender and stuff, for their market stall. My mom does it sometimes with hydrangea flowers."

"Ohhhh."

Sarai knelt beside her son, said a blessing over his head, and hugged him. "How do you feel, my love? How is your ankle?"

It was bound up in some kind of bandage. Isaac moved it uncomfortably. "Much the same. Thank you." He was still looking over her shoulder at the new arrivals. "But—"

Sarai smiled. "'Yes, your cousins have arrived! And their timing could not have been better!'"

Isaac sat up straighter and grinned at them. "Abigail and Nathan?" He held out his hands. Nadeem and Ava came forward to take them. "Welcome, cousins." He squeezed their fingers and let go. "Thank Hashem for bringing you when we need you so much!"

Sarai took down some supplies from a shelf, returned to her son's side, and began changing his bandage. "I know you were feeling guilty about Ester being forced to fill in for you at the market, Isaac, so you may put your mind at rest now. Nathan is here to assist me. Your sister and Abigail can remain here to tend to you. They will be excellent companions."

A noise at the doorway told them Ester had returned. She put the jug down on the floor, handling it with more effort now that it was full. "Mother," Ester said, "Isaac has not been without company. You know our neighbors promised to check on him. Isaac, didn't the widow Alkana check in on you while we were gone?"

"Twice!" her brother declared.

Sarai said, "A better neighbor never lived. Isaac, did the widow Alkana also take our tagine pot over to cook in the community oven, as I asked?"

He assured her that she had.

"Good. Otherwise there would be no dinner waiting for us. And with our extra company tonight, I'm glad I used the large stew pot instead of the small. Very well, children, now we will wash." She gestured toward the water jug.

"You sure need it," Ava remarked to Nadeem. "You're covered in dirt."

"Good thing you can't see yourself," he retorted.

Ava would've loved a shower—or a dip in that beautiful Sabtah river. But she worked with what she had, rubbing water across her face and washing her hands in a bowl that Ester filled for them, while Sarai took another wash bowl to Isaac. When everyone was more or less clean, Sarai got Nadeem to help Isaac stand up and hop over to the colorful rug in the center of the room. "Afternoon prayer time!" she announced.

As he propped up Isaac by one shoulder, Nadeem gave Ava an uncertain look. He'd been around for occasional afternoon prayers at Granny Buena's house, listening respectfully and with appreciation, but he'd never said the words aloud. Would the family here notice?

"Gather round and face east, toward Jerusalem!" Sarai shooed them together like a flock of sheep. "Nathan, as our honored guest, would you like to lead us?"

Worst case scenario! Ava thought, *Help!*

Then Nadeem said simply, "Thank you, Aunt Sarai, but I would rather hear Isaac do it."

To Ava's relief, no one questioned this.

Isaac began the Hebrew prayers, standing on one leg between his mother and Nadeem with his hurt ankle hanging awkwardly in the air. His voice was beautiful, and he even hit the plaintive up-and-down notes that Ava knew were especially hard to sing. He ended with the *Aleinu*:

It is our duty to praise the Master of all, to acclaim the greatness of the One who forms all creation . . .

Ava whispered to Nadeem. "It's amazing—we sing this same exact prayer in our time, a thousand years later!"

Nadeem's eyes were like stars. He whispered back, "Yeah! And the same words are in the Qur'an!"

The thought was awe-inspiring. But it also reminded Ava of how far she and Nadeem had traveled—in time *and* space. She added an extra prayer in her heart: *Please, let us get safely home.*

CHAPTER 9

After prayers, Sarai said, "Girls, the sun will soon be going down. Would you run and pick up our evening meal?" She pointed toward a large, sturdy basket with double handles that stood against the far wall.

"Of course," Ava said, grabbing the basket. Ester simply strode over to the doorway in silence and put her sandals back on.

Once they were out in the street, Ester complained to Ava, "Did you notice? My mother couldn't wait to get rid of me. I think she wants to talk to Isaac without me there."

"Why would she want to do that?"

Ester stopped and looked her in the eye, like she was trying to read Ava's mind.

Ava hoped she couldn't.

"Can I trust you, cousin?" Ester finally said.

"Of course!"

"No, I mean really trust you. Life or death. I know that's a lot to ask, but we are family."

Ava knew what was coming. "Yes! I'm here for you. Tell me what's wrong."

Ester paused for a moment, trembling a little. Then the whole story of Bedir and Prince Abdur Rahman came pouring out in an urgent whisper. By the end of it, Ester's eyes were swimming with tears. "I want our family to help Bedir and the prince, but my mother never listens to me. She favors my brother always, and she treats me like a silly child."

Ava felt heaviness in her heart. She hugged Ester tight. "You know what? Your mom relies on you for everything and actually treats you like an adult, even though she may not realize it. I mean—*get the water, Ester; get fish for our dinner, Ester; go get whatever it is from the community oven, Ester.* If she didn't know she could trust you, she wouldn't be giving you all that responsibility. Right?"

Ester put down the big basket and dried her eyes on a loose woven sleeve. "I suppose."

Ava patted her shoulder. "I think things will

work out for Prince Abdur Rahman. And I'll be your friend through all this, okay?"

Ester nodded.

Ava smiled. "Nad—uh, Nathan will stand by you too. You're not alone. Now let's go get the food before everyone starts wondering what's taking so long."

"Yes, yes. Thank you, cousin." Ester gave her a genuine, warm smile. "I'm sorry I was a bit unwelcoming to you earlier. I'm glad you've come."

Ava hugged her again, and they hurried off to the community oven, which turned out to be a beehive-shaped structure made of clay. The two girls joined a line of several other girls and women, who all knew Ester. When they learned who Ava was, they immediately started offering suggestions for sight-seeing and asking questions about her family back home that Ava wasn't sure how to answer. She gave Ester a *Help me!* look.

Ester laughed. "Give my cousin some space to breathe, my friends."

"Next!" The call came from the baker, a hearty woman who wore her hair tied back in a scarf. For each customer, she lifted the giant oven lid, slapped about ten thin ovals of dough against the brick oven wall, and turned them quickly over with a paddle to bake them on both sides. Then, still using her paddle, the baker scraped up the fragrant flatbreads and slid them into the cloth that each woman in line held open.

When it was Ester's turn, she deftly caught the bread that slid off of the baker's paddle into her cloth. Then she tied a knot at the top of the cloth and handed it to Ava. "Hold on to this for a moment. Our stew is waiting for us over here," she said, moving toward a firepit where a group of many clay pots with cone-shaped lids rested upon hot stones. What had Sarai called those pots—tagines?

Ester gave a coin and a smile to the boy standing beside the firepit. "Thank you," she told him. "Blessings on your family." Then she pulled some more cloth from the basket, wrapped her hands in it to protect against the blistering heat, and picked up a pot that was decorated with painted blue flowers. Ava noticed that each pot in the firepit had unique glazed designs so the women could tell which one belonged to whom.

After Ester wedged the tagine inside the carrier, Ava put the bread bundle on top. Then each girl took a handle to carry it carefully back to the house.

The delicious smell suddenly made Ava feel a thousand years' worth of hungry. Her stomach let out an embarrassing, loud rumble.

Ester chuckled, and Ava joined in.

Something had definitely changed between them, Ava realized. They were really, truly becoming friends.

CHAPTER 10

When they returned to the house with the heavy food basket, Ava was surprised to see that Sarai, Isaac, and Nadeem had been joined by Aunt Devora, Uncle Yosef, and two unfamiliar men. And they were all seated cross-legged in a wide circle on the beautiful living room rug.

Oh wow! Ava realized. *In Sabtah, people eat without a table or chairs!*

"Greetings and blessings, Shalom and Salaam!" Aunt Devora called to the girls as they entered. "We've brought more family to meet you, Abigail!"

The others on the rug echoed Aunt Devora's kindly words. Ava nodded and smiled at everyone as she and Ester lowered their burden to the floor.

Sarai came rushing forward to help. "Thank

you, my dears, and may Hashem bless the meal you bring us."

The hanging oil lamp had been lit, and it cast a homey glow throughout the room. Sarai had laid out clay dishes and some basins for handwashing on the rug, but there were no knives or forks and only one big spoon, which Ava figured was for serving.

Ava and Ester helped Sarai arrange the food in the center of the circle. Ava placed the heavenly-fragrant, cloth-wrapped stack of breads alongside the tagine pot and untied the knot. Ahhh! A burst of tantalizing bread-scented steam rose into the air, and everyone around the rug made sounds of appreciation.

Sarai motioned both girls to sit, then retrieved the fresh fish Ester had bought in the market and dropped it inside the pot to steam. "The fish will be cooked by the time we have finished the hand-washing," she said.

"A blessing upon the hands that made this food," said Uncle Yosef, beginning to wash.

"A blessing upon all of us here!" cried one of the other men, washing with water from the basin nearest him and passing it on to the man beside him. Then he nodded at Ava and Nadeem. "Abigail and Nathan, a special blessing upon you as travelers: may the Lord defend you from harm and bring you home safe at journey's end. Abigail, I am Sabatai Behnamú, cousin to Ester and Isaac's father, and this is my brother-in-law, Avraham Alhadeff."

Next came another prayer, the traditional blessing Ava's own family said before every dinner. *Baruch atah Adonai* . . .

Ava looked around at the friendly faces as Sarai doled out the stew. Sarai must have called them all here to discuss Bedir and the Muslim prince, but none of them looked worried or sad in this moment. A familiar warmth washed over her: a sense of belonging.

Nadeem whispered his usual *bismillah*. He scooped up his first bite of stew in a folded piece of bread, as if the bread were a spoon. Then, his mouth full, he blurted, "I think this may be the best thing I've ever tasted in my life!"

Ava liked strawberry ice cream better, but she knew exactly what Nadeem meant. Both she and Nadeem came from households where the cooking was phenomenal. But this simple food was a different level of taste experience. "It's fantastic! What's in it?" she asked Aunt Sarai.

Sarai's face lit up with pride. "Well, let's see . . . chickpeas, fava beans, olives, almonds, onions and apricots, and of course, my secret blend of spices."

Ava said impulsively, "I'm so glad we came to Sabtah."

Everyone around the rug laughed. "Well, Sarai," Aunt Devora said, "it seems young Abigail hopes to learn cooking from you while she's here! We won't mention this to her mother!"

The meal continued in this lighthearted way as the sky outside grew darker. Then Sarai said to Ester: "Dear, please take your cousins outside and wait until I call you back in."

Ava murmured to Nadeem, "If Ester has to leave, how come Isaac gets to stay? Is it because he's 'the man of the family' with his dad away in Spain?"

Nadeem shrugged. "Maybe it's because of his ankle."

Judging by Ester's clenched jaw, Ava didn't think so. But the proud girl obeyed her mother without protest.

It was excruciating to have to leave the room when something so important was going on. But Ava couldn't think of one single thing to do about it.

The three of them emerged into the quiet street,

and Ava looked up. Then she gasped, forgetting all about Bedir, the prince, the Button Box, and anything else but the astonishing sight of the ancient night sky.

The stars were so brilliant that they might as well have been tiny light bulbs. It seemed like the constellations actually hung lower than they did back home, as if Ava could reach out and pluck them and string them round her neck like luminous pearls. There were hundreds . . . thousands . . . gazillions of them.

She heard Nadeem utter an exclamation. She was pretty sure it was "Mash'Allah!"

"What is it?" Ester took her hand.

Ava couldn't answer. She was still in awe.

It was Nadeem who found his voice first. "Ester, both of us have just noticed something. We've come so far from home, even the stars look different."

Ester squeezed Ava's hand. "The stars may change, but hearts do not. As long as you're both in Sabtah, I'll do whatever I can to help you feel at home, cousins. We are family."

For another long moment, the three of them stared up at the sky together.

Then Ava asked Ester, "What do you think is going on in there?"

With a question in her eyes, Ester tilted her head meaningfully at Nadeem.

Nadeem noticed. "Oh, if you're wondering whether I know that Bedir asked your mother for help with Prince Abdur Rahman today, the answer is yes. Aunt Sarai talked to your brother about it while you and Ava were out getting dinner, and I couldn't help but hear them."

"I knew it!" Ester cried. "Mother wanted Isaac's advice, but she didn't respect mine. And now Isaac gets to stay inside with the adults while we have to wait out here."

"Well," Ava said weakly, "Isaac is older than the rest of us."

"Not by much." Ester kicked at a stone, then fell silent.

"So?" Ava nudged her with an elbow. "What do you think they're talking about right now?"

"They're probably weighing the risks," Ester said at last. "And there's definitely a huge risk to all of us if we get involved. If our family takes Prince Abdur Rahman to Spain, his enemies may find out that we organized the prince's escape. Then they would take revenge upon every Jew in Sabtah."

Ava shuddered. The thought of anything bad

happening to the people here was unbearable. No wonder Sarai had been so troubled by Bedir's request.

"It's a hard decision," Nadeem remarked. "For what it's worth, Abigail and I are on your side. We think there's no other choice but to step in and do something to save the prince's life."

"Thank you, cousins."

An uneasy silence fell again.

About half an hour later, Sarai let them back into the house and the other adults took their leave, with many fond blessings.

"Mother," Ester said after the door closed behind the last visitor, "I spoke to my cousins about the prince. They have the right to know, for whatever action we take will affect them too."

Isaac, who was still sitting on the rug, spoke up. "Yes—we must all agree!"

Sarai gave Ava and Nadeem a concerned half smile. "My dears, I am not sure your parents would have sent you to stay with us if they knew what danger awaited you in Sabtah. If you wish to return to your parents in Tangiers so as not to be mixed up in all this, I will send you first thing tomorrow.."

"Please don't send us away," Nadeem said. "I think we would shame the family if we left while you were in trouble. We'll see this through together."

Ava added, "No matter what."

Sarai's smile became warmer. "You are good young people, indeed. But let me know if you change your minds. The fact is—after talking it over this evening, our family has resolved to aid the prince. Now we must pray that the Most High will help us stay safe while we do so."

Ava gulped. "Our minds won't change."

"How will the escape be managed?" Ester asked.

"Tomorrow night, Sabatai Benhamú will take Bedir and Prince Abdur Rahman across the Mediterranean Sea to Jabal Tāriq in his boat, under cover of darkness."

That sounded simple enough.

Ester exclaimed, "I'm glad to hear it! May Hashem guide him."

While Sarai and Ester started gathering up the dinner dishes, Nadeem whispered to Ava, "Okay, we're one step closer to completing our mission! Now what?"

Ava felt the sudden warm, fuzzy pressure of Sheba wrapping around her ankles. She bent over and scooped her up. "Hey," she whispered to the cat. "How can we help with the big getaway plan? Give us a hint!" But Sheba simply purred and closed her eyes, giving off "Who, me? I'm just a regular house pet" vibes.

Nadeem said to Sheba, "You are one stubborn cat." Sheba flicked a stiff tail at him.

He kept speaking to Ava in an undertone. "Well, there's one thing we know for sure: you and I should stay together, every single minute. If weird things start happening, they're going to happen fast, and we shouldn't be apart when they do. We should both be at the market tomorrow when Bedir shows up."

"Right." Ava set Sheba on the floor and approached Sarai, who was giving Ester instructions about how to wash the tagine properly. "Excuse me, Aunt Sarai. May I please come along to the market again in the morning?"

Sarai looked unsure, but Isaac offered support. "Mother, do let Ester show Cousin Abigail some more of Sabtah before you shut them up with me here," he said. "I'll be perfectly happy here at home with Sheba and the widow Alkana and all our other neighbors."

Sarai gave in more easily than Ava had expected. "You're right, Isaac. Where is my hospitality? My brother would be most unhappy with me if I leave

Abigail behind on her first full day here." She turned to Ava. "Of course, my dear, you may stay close to your brother until you've gotten used to this new place. Ester can keep you company; I should have thought of that myself. But as you know, I've had a great deal on my mind."

So the next morning, all three kids set off for the marketplace with Sarai, Aunt Devora, and Uncle Yosef. As soon as they set up the stall, Sarai put Nadeem in Ester's place at the herb and spice table. Ava and Ester leaned against the nearby wall to watch, just as they had done the day before.

"Do you know what this is?" Sarai tested Nadeem by taking a delicate pinch of a thready red spice and holding it up to his nose.

"Saffron!" he exclaimed. "I love this stuff! My mother tells me it's very expensive because it's hard to get. It comes from the center of rare orchid flowers, right?"

"Well done, nephew."

"Hmph. Saffron is easy," Ester commented to Ava in a low voice. "The color and smell are so distinctive!"

As the marketplace grew busier, Nadeem called out to the passing shoppers. "Come buy our fine saffron, honored brothers and sisters! How can you make delicious couscous without precious saffron? Throw in some fish, and you can call it a day," he urged.

To Ava's surprise, this hustle seemed to be working.

A crowd formed and began to move in their direction. Among them were some men in finely worked yet travel-worn embroidered robes. They were—hey, wait a second—they were pushing some of the local people. Voices were raised. That didn't seem right. All that fuss over saffron?

"Oh no." Ester grabbed Ava's arm.

"Ouch!" Ava yelped. "What is it?"

Ester looked hopeless and angry at the same time. "Hashem preserve. All that planning last night was for nothing, Abigail. They've found him!"

Ava didn't need to ask who.

CHAPTER 11

The restless crowd formed an uneasy circle around two distinctive figures. One was Bedir, in his easily recognizable Greek tunic. The other was a tall man in a brown hooded cloak. His arm was bent in a way that made Ava suspect he was holding the hilt of a weapon at his waist, hidden under his robes.

This had to be Prince Abdur Rahman. Yet in spite of his danger, the prince's lean, intense face didn't show anger or even fear. He looked . . . sorrowful.

Suddenly, a skinny teenage guy with a sloppy white turban shot forward from the crowd. His embroidered robe swirled as he snatched at the tall man's brown hood, which fell backward to reveal a strong profile framed by dark hair with unusual streaks of auburn.

"I knew it!" shouted the teenager, whose scraggly beard reminded Ava of Theo, her spelling tutor back home. "It's Prince Abdur Rahman! The rumors are true—he's alive!"

"Who are *you*?" demanded someone else in the crowd, giving the Theo-type teenager a suspicious look. "I've never seen you in Sabtah before."

"That's not important!" snapped the Theo-guy. "Aren't you listening? I just told you the Prince of the Umayyads is in your midst! Don't you know what kind of reward the royal Abbasids are offering for his capture?"

Ava's heart turned to ice.

By this point, everyone in the market was staring at Abdur Rahman. The word "prince" flew from lip to lip.

Ester's mother gasped, "Holy Lord of Abraham, protect him! He will never get out of Sabtah alive!"

Nadeem left his post at the table to join Ava and Ester. "If the prince never escapes Sabtah," he whispered in Ava's ear, "the great Golden Age of Spain won't happen. Ester won't move to his court. Her whole life will probably be different. If she's really our ancestor, you and I might never even be born. We've got to save Abdur Rahman!"

If this were a movie, Ava thought, she and Nadeem would whip out super-weapons and take on the entire crowd by themselves. But this was reality. She was stumped and scared.

She could do nothing but watch as a very old man in a complicated wow of a headdress came forward and poked a knobbly finger into the Theo-guy's middle. "If this is indeed the Prince of the Umayyads, how dare you lay hands upon him? He must have come here to seek refuge among the people of his mother, Ra'ha—Berbers like us. We will not betray our kin!"

"Then you're fools!" the Theo-guy retorted. "But suit yourselves. If you don't help bring him in, that will mean a bigger share of the reward for the rest of us!" He pointed at several rugged-looking travelers who seemed to be with him. There were too many of them for Abdur Rahman and Bedir to fend off in a fight.

More people of Sabtah began to speak, siding with the old man in the headdress. But the bounty hunter guys were much louder and more aggressive than these reasonable folks.

"Cousins," Ester said, "that is the prince whom some would say should become caliph, leader of the faithful of Islam. And he has asked us for help. What can we do for him?"

What *could* they do? Ava certainly couldn't think of a way to talk the bounty hunters into giving up their prey. Her mind flashed back to her standoff with her classmate Fern on the way home from school. That was as close as she had ever come to getting in a real fight, and she wasn't especially proud of how she'd handled the situation. She and Nadeem and even the brave Ester wouldn't be much use in a brawl against a bunch of adults.

"I got nothing," Nadeem admitted.

"Neither do I. Ester, you live here—do you have any ideas?" Ava asked.

"Yes," was the calm reply. Ester stood and quickly moved close to Sarai. "Mother. Don't panic, please, but I'm going to borrow a boat and take the prince and his friend Bedir to Spain. Right now. There's no time to lose."

"Ester! You can't!" Sarai gasped.

"Oh, indeed I can." There was a small, grim smile on Ester's lips. "You know how easy it is to get from here to the port of Jabal Tāriq. I could do it in the dark with one hand stuck in a clay jar."

Sarai's forehead wrinkled with fear. "But my

daughter, how can you accomplish it out in the open like this, with the prince's enemies gathered? Look at them—think of what they might do if you were caught! All the Jews in Sabtah could end up paying dearly for your actions."

Ester seemed unmoved. "I know the risks. But doesn't the Scripture say, *Thou shalt not stand idly by the blood of thy neighbor*? Give this crowd a few more minutes, and the blood of the prince—and of Bedir too—will be on our consciences." She gestured at the terrible scene developing in front of them. The Berber elder who wanted the prince left alone had gathered a larger following, but the bounty hunters were gradually pushing them away, closing in on their intended victim.

Ava hoped the locals would be able to keep the bounty hunters back, but it sure didn't look like that would happen.

Nadeem chimed in, "Ester's right. We have to at least try to rescue him, Aunt Sarai!"

As her mother visibly wavered, Ester pressed her advantage. "I'll hide my face so I won't be recognized," she declared. "No one will know I'm a Jew. And as you're so fond of pointing out, Mother, I'm small. Everyone will think I'm a child. No one pays attention to children, which means no one will be able to connect our family with Abdur Rahman's escape. The Jews of Sabtah will be safe."

Sarai suddenly seemed to deflate. She kissed her daughter's cheek and said, "Go, my Ester! Take this token Bedir gave me. It will mark you as someone the prince can trust." Tears running down her cheeks, she attached a jeweled silver-and-ruby pin to the inside of Ester's robe.

The button of Abdur Rahman!

Ava cried, "You're not going alone, cousin. Nathan and I are coming with you!"

Ester threw her an unexpected, genuine grin. "All right. We'll borrow old Malik Sodi's boat. He doesn't use it to fish anymore, but it's perfectly sound. I'll go get it ready to set sail, while you bring the prince and Bedir to me."

Sure, no problem, Ava thought with desperate sarcasm.

Nadeem asked, "Where's the boat exactly?"

"Do you see the very last building on the wharf over there?" Ester pointed. "Behind that building, you'll find a wooden dock. I'll be waiting there in the boat that has a carved monkey for a figurehead."

Before Ava and Nadeem had even finished nodding, Ester pulled her headscarf forward to hide her eyes and wrapped the bottom folds of the cloth around her mouth. Then she dashed off toward the dock.

CHAPTER 12

Nadeem and Ava went in the opposite direction, squeezing their way into the group surrounding the prince. Several people broke away from the crowd and hurried off, seemingly unwilling to be involved in the violence that was about to break out. The Theo-guy and a few other bounty hunters pulled out long, wicked knives and began to lunge at the prince and his loyal friend, who now stood back-to-back, circling as they retreated down the street.

One man yelled, "Most noble prince! Do you want to escape the country? I'll take you, if you pay me in gold!"

An old woman hurrying away called over her shoulder at the man: "Shame on you! Taking money for a life! *Audhu billah!*"

Ignoring the old woman, another man shouted, "Come to my tent! I will hide you, for a fee."

Ava hoped the prince wouldn't be foolish enough to believe any of these offers.

Bedir tried to calm everyone down. "This man is not who you think he is. We are simple travelers. You're making a terrible mistake. Let us go in peace."

Good luck with that! Ava thought.

While Bedir pleaded, the prince pivoted in silence, sizing up the threat. Ava figured he was trying to decide what to do. She and Nadeem had to reach him before he made the wrong choice.

"Duck and dodge!" Nadeem whispered to Ava. This was a touch-football move they used at school. Quick and slick as licked gummy worms, they crouched low and zigzagged their way through the gathering.

Ava ended up right next to Abdur Rahman. She whispered, "Your Highness! Your friend Bedir asked my family to take you to Spain. Come with us! A boat is waiting."

The brown, weary eyes focused on Ava. There was no trust in them. Why should there be?

Yet she knew exactly how to change that. She

pushed aside her robe to uncover the gleaming silver-and-ruby pin from the Button Box.

She held her breath, hoping he'd recognize it. After all, it was the same pin that Bedir had given Sarai—the same pin Ester was wearing right now. Time travel really was wild.

It will mark you as someone the prince can trust, Sarai had told Ester.

The prince's face lit up as though Ava had just flipped a switch. "Little loyal one," he declared, "you and your people shall learn the gratitude of the Umayyads. I'll follow where you lead. But first— stand back!"

Whoosh! He drew an enormous sword and held it up, poised for action, in a confident stance that spoke of years of experience. The hot sun reflected off the sword's polished blade with searing brightness. The silver handle dazzled with the gleam of red jewels, the same rubies as those on the button Ava wore.

"In the name of the Most High!" the prince thundered in a deep and powerful voice.

Abdur Rahman's sudden transformation from humble traveler to fierce warrior was apparently more than the bounty hunters bargained for. They hesitated, their knives wavering. But only for a moment. Then they charged forward again.

"Run!" Nadeem pulled on Ava's hand. They darted through an opening in the crowd and headed straight for the building at the end of the wharf. Ava's long robes threatened to trip her, so she hitched them above her ankles as she sped up.

Behind them, she could hear Bedir and the prince following.

Yells went up as the bounty hunters gave chase. Clanging, sword-type noises filled the air.

Ava had never run this fast, not even during the unbearable 100-yard dash in PE. Her legs began to ache. "Don't look back, Nadeem!" she cried. "Keep going!" She hoped Abdur Rahman and Bedir were still right behind them.

"There!" Nadeem pointed. "The dock!"

Ava saw the boat with the carved wooden monkey. It was held in place by a rope tied to a metal ring on the dock. Ester waited on board, standing at the tiller, just as she'd promised.

"Faster, faster!" Ester cried. "They're gaining on you!" She'd already hoisted the sail, which was filling with a stiff breeze. The craft strained against the rope that held it to the dock.

Ava's breath was ragged, and her chest hurt. She jumped over the foot or two of salt water between the dock and the boat, landing on the boat's deck. After a small stumble, she regained her balance. A moment later, Nadeem leaped aboard, followed by Bedir.

But the prince was still farther back, fighting off bounty hunters. Bedir leaned over the railing and bellowed, "Your Highness! Make an end!"

Abdur Rahman gave one last mighty sweep of his sword, forcing his attackers to jump back. Then he whirled around and ran at full tilt toward Bedir's outstretched hands.

"Whoa! Look at him run!" Nadeem cried. "He's like the Usain Bolt of ancient times."

"Hurry!" Ava and Ester shrieked.

The prince leaped into the air and hurled himself onto the boat. Bedir steadied him. Then, with a slash of his sword, Abdur Rahman sliced through the rope tying the boat to the dock. Ester moved the tiller, and the fishing vessel bounded forward into the sea. With the wind already swelling the sails, it seemed as if they would make a clean and quick getaway.

But one determined bounty hunter jumped off the end of the pier and grabbed hold of the monkey on the boat's stern. He dangled there for a second, his feet in the air, and then began to scramble up the side.

The prince's sword rose once more.

Ava and Nadeem covered their eyes.

"*Argghhh!*"

There was a splash, and Ava heard Abdur Rahman slide his sword back into its sheath.

She opened her eyes.

The would-be abductor was swimming back to the dock, sputtering and moaning.

Whew. She'd thought for a minute that Abdur Rahman might have killed him.

"*Alhamdulilah!* The prince is a good guy," Nadeem whispered. His voice was shaky. He'd obviously also expected a much more drastic outcome for the greedy man.

As the boat pulled away from land, the mob howled in fury and shook their fists, staffs and knives in the air. But happier voices on shore shouted "*Allahu Akbar!*" in gratitude to God for the prince's escape.

The cheers, curses, and threats from the dock grew faint as the wind and Ester's sailing skill carried them farther out to sea.

"We did it!" Ester shouted.

"*You* did it, Ester!" Ava cried. "Your plan worked!"

Bedir's face radiated relief. "Well done, young people. We are deeply grateful. My trust in your family was well placed." He turned to the prince. "Your Highness, these are the children of the Jewish family I spoke of—Ester and her cousins Abigail and Nathan."

Abdur Rahman placed his hand on his heart as he faced each of them in turn. "Ester, Abigail, and Nathan, you have shown great courage. May the blessings of the Most High shower upon you like water from His heaven. I am deeply in your debt."

Ester exclaimed, "Your Highness, you owe us nothing! We Jews are commanded to save the lives of the innocent."

"Seriously, it was our honor to help, Your Highness," Nadeem added.

Ava felt too shy to speak. Then she remembered what Granny Buena always said. "It is our way," she declared.

"Children, you are admirable and modest in spirit," said Abdur Rahman. "I shall not allow your courage to go unrewarded. Perhaps I may someday be in a position be to honor you with gold, jewels, and great favor. For now, you have my blessing and the grateful prayers of one who will never forget what you have done."

"Thank you, Your Highness," Ester said, keeping a firm grip on the tiller. "We don't need a reward, now or ever. That isn't why we helped. Your blessing is more precious than gold or diamonds."

Ava instantly felt a little guilty, because she'd been enjoying the idea of Abdur Rahman presenting Ester's family with treasure chests full of heavy coins and glittering jewels.

She tried to focus instead on the prince's blessings. Blessings were good.

Less shiny, but good.

"Besides," Ester added, "going to Spain is no hardship for us. I love it there, and my cousins told me yesterday they've been longing to see it for themselves."

"Ah!" Bedir the Greek beamed at them. "This was a lucky chance indeed, then!"

Abdur Rahman raised a hand in the air. "Bedir, where you see luck, I see the guiding hand of the Most High. As we are told, *He is above all comprehension yet is acquainted with all things.*"

Ester smiled and nodded.

If Ava and Nadeem had learned anything from their unusual family, it was that when Muslims and Jews spoke of the Most High, whether they called him Allah or Hashem, they were speaking of the same God. For all the deep and important differences in their faiths, this common thread had always existed between them. So it was no surprise that Ester and the prince understood each other so well.

"My father happens to be in Spain right now," Ester told the prince. "Once we get there, my cousins and I can seek him out and stay under his protection until the mood calms down in Sabtah."

"Oh, good point," said Ava as it dawned on her. "The guys who attacked the prince might be watching for this boat to come back. We'll probably be safer if we lie low in Spain for a few days, until they leave town."

"You see, Your Highness?" Ester's teeth flashed bright. "We are content."

Nadeem said, not very enthusiastically, "Sure, sure. Who needs treasure? A trip to Spain in a small fishing boat is way better than gold and jewels."

The prince's dark eyes lit up. "Well, young ones, since your hearts are so set upon Spain, the land of

Spain is what I shall hope to give to you. If ever I rule there, you may join me, with your parents and your kin. You shall live upon my lands or in my royal house and be my honored courtiers. In fact, I pledge to you now: every Jew shall be safe in my realm."

CHAPTER 13

No one knew what to say for a minute. Ava couldn't believe the prince had made such a huge promise. It couldn't really be that easy, could it?

Finally, Ester gasped, "Thank you!"

Abdur Rahman smiled warmly. Then he beckoned to Ava and Nadeem. "Time for a rest," he said. He moved aside his sword and lowered himself to the boat's deck, then leaned his back against the craft's curved side.

After so much excitement, Ava and Nadeem were glad to join him. Bedir, too, sat down, though he did so with a groan: "Oh, my aging bones!"

The prince passed around a flask of water that he took from his belt. He said to Ester, "I sincerely regret that I cannot take your place at the tiller, so that you could rest here in my place. But neither

Bedir nor I have any skill with water craft."

Ester took a drink from the flask and handed it to Nadeem. "I'm not tired, Your Highness. You're the ones who had to run across town and fight off a mob! All I had to do was wait here on the boat. Just be sure to duck if I have to shift our sailing direction, or the wooden beam at the bottom of the sail will swing across the deck and hit you. After you've survived so many dangers, it would be a pity to lose you to the boom of a fishing boat."

While the others laughed at this, Ava was thinking about the contented, friendly people she'd met in the Jewish Quarter last night. The Jews had built a close, strong community in Sabtah. It was hard to imagine that they'd really uproot their lives to move to an unfamiliar place just because one guy said they would be welcome. It would seem like a giant risk to them. And Ava wouldn't blame them. What if something else went wrong, and history didn't turn out the way Granny had said it did?

Ava gathered up the courage to ask a question. "Prince . . . I mean, Your Highness . . ."

He sensed her hesitation. "Yes?"

"You said that our family will be welcome in your kingdom."

"If the Most High grants me a kingdom. And I will admit that right now such a future seems unlikely, child. But I do not make the promise lightly."

"I believe what you say, Your Highness. But how can you be sure that your people will accept us? Would they treat Jews well, even when . . . um . . . when you're not around?" She couldn't help thinking of the many stories she'd heard and read about how wherever Jews went, throughout history, they seemed to encounter people who misunderstood and mistreated them.

Abdur Rahman didn't seem surprised or offended by the question. "You're wise beyond your years, young Abigail. I understand why you ask this. If your people take the enormous step of joining mine in Spain, your welcome should not rely solely upon the word of one man. For kings and caliphs may command the flesh, but the heart cannot be so swayed, and if my people were against you in their hearts, you could never truly be safe with us."

Ava nodded. He understood her fears—maybe even better than she did herself.

"Be assured," Abdur Rahman continued solemnly. "Though each human is by nature an imperfect follower, the true way of Islam is to promote peace among the peoples of the earth. Our destiny is harmony, not division."

Ava's shoulders relaxed. This was the kind of thing she would love to talk over and think about with her friends Eliza and Rochelle. As soon as she got a chance, she would.

Now Nadeem had a question. "Uh, Your Highness, I noticed back in Sabtah that you didn't use your sword until those guys forced you to. You didn't get mad. You seemed totally calm. How did you do it? Abigail and I have been attacked just for being who we are, and it's hard not to lose control."

Oh. So Ava wasn't the only one thinking of their conflict with Fern at school.

Abdur Rahman's smile grew wistful. "I may have seemed calm, Nathan, but my spirit was in great turmoil. As my respected mother once told me, it helps to remember that those who hurt and betray are numerous and deep as the sands outside holy Mecca. And like the sands, they are beneath us—though they may burn the soles of our feet. The burning serves as a reminder to travel as quickly and as lightly over these threats as possible on the way to our blessed destination. Do not let enemies, or the foolish, distract or dissuade you. Keep your eyes on the right path."

"But sometimes you can't ignore them," Ava pointed out. "You had to fight those bounty hunters in the end. They wouldn't have left you alone otherwise."

There was a moment of quiet, broken only by the flapping of the breeze in the sail and the creaking of the ropes holding the rigging.

Abdur Rahman sighed. "Ah, children. Always, always, attacks will come to us, often when we least expect them. But I believe Allah the Merciful balances such betrayal by inspiring others to come to our aid in surprising ways. Take my faithful Bedir, for example." He waved a hand toward the other man. "He was once my tutor. Now he is my friend and protector. He is not of my people or my faith, yet he has saved my life countless times—as you did today. You were bystanders, and now you've become heroes. The harm that hatred does in the world will finally stop when all bystanders decide to become heroes instead of onlookers."

"Insh'Allah!" said Nadeem enthusiastically.

Ava's heart agreed. If the bystanders of the world refused to stand by anymore, bullies wouldn't have a chance.

"As my father would say: *If the cucumbers would rise*

up together, they could vanquish the bad gardener," Ester put in helpfully.

Ava looked at Nadeem.

Nadeem looked at Ava.

Well, it was official: now they knew that Granny Buena's love for quirky old proverbs ran in the family.

"The wind has changed," Ester called. "Heads down, everyone!"

She gave a sharp pull on the tiller. The boom swung across the boat, the slack sail rippling. Ava felt slightly queasy watching Ester re-tighten the ropes while the canvas ballooned out again.

"No broken skulls?" Ester asked.

"We're fine!" Ava assured her. No way was she going to complain about being seasick in this boat full of super-people.

"Good!" Ester said. "We're on course, and the wind's in the right direction. If this keeps up, we should arrive at the port of Jabal Tāriq in a few hours."

Bedir cleared his throat. His cheeks turned pink. "Actually, I wasn't quite straightforward with you when I said our destination was Jabal Tāriq, Ester. You see, I wasn't yet sure I could trust you."

Ester threw a sharp glance at the Greek over her shoulder. Ava's stomach felt queasy again.

"Oh!" The prince raised his eyebrows at his friend. "I was not aware that you had misled them, Bedir."

Bedir explained, "It is true that we will pass close to Jabal Tāriq, young friends, but our final destination lies farther eastward."

"So where are we actually headed?" Nadeem asked.

"Almuñécar."

Ester looked startled. "Why?"

Ava suspected that this place was much farther than Ester had bargained for.

The prince explained. "Long ago, my grandfather of blessed memory, Caliph Hisham ibn Abd al-Malik, sent thousands of his soldiers into Spain—to Almuñécar. Their many descendants now await me there, where my arrival will be kept secret and Bedir and I will be safe. The three of you shall be safe there as well, if you are willing to take us that far." He eyed Bedir again. "However, since the truth was not told you, there would be no loss of honor in refusing to do so. You may take us to Jabal Tāriq and we shall disembark there, to make our way to Almuñécar on foot."

Ester hesitated for a moment.

Nadeem quickly put in, "I think we should make sure the prince is completely safe and take him where he needs to go. Don't you, Cousin Ester?"

Ava added, "Or all this would have been for nothing."

Ester squared her shoulders and said, "Agreed. We shall go to Almuñécar. If the weather holds, we should reach it later tonight. We're committed to this venture, aren't we, cousins?"

Nadeem gave Ava a meaningful nod.

Ava wondered what this meant for their mission. Would their work in the past be done once the prince reached Spain? Or was there even more for them to accomplish? Maybe she and Nadeem were supposed to hang out with Ester till she met up with her dad, which seemed like it was going to take much more effort than she'd expected.

Twenty-four hours ago, Ava had been desperate to get back home. But now, the thought of sticking around a little longer was actually kind of exciting. She would love to see the prince meet his allies. And it could be fun to let Ester show her the Spain she adored so much.

Placing a hand on his chest, Abdur Rahman said, "Thank you, young people. You are courageous as well as honorable." Then the prince brought his long, strong fingers together in an almost prayerful attitude and said in a thoughtful voice, "Abigail and Nathan, you have asked me questions that were important to you. Know that I, too, have spent much time questioning. It is the only way to find enlightenment."

"So we learn in the Torah," Ester confirmed.

"I ask questions of myself and of the Most High," Abdur Rahman continued. "Ever since my family's rule in the lands of Islam was overthrown, I wonder: Can I be sure that this path before me is a rightly guided path? Can I be certain that what I do in Spain is not for vengeance against the Abbasids or for my own personal glory, but for the good of my people, and in accordance with the Most High?"

His musings fell into a deep silence.

And that's when it happened.

A spark inside Ava fluttered to life. She caught her breath, wondering, *What is this?*

All she knew was that, deep inside, she felt the urge to do something. Prince Abdur Rahman had asked questions, and she—regular Ava—was being offered the chance to give him answers.

She could turn away from this moment. Do nothing and say nothing. But Granny had told her to look for opportunities to mend the world. This felt like one of those opportunities. *I'll do it.*

She stood and looked down at the prince. When she opened her mouth, fancy words poured forth in a strange voice like a sweet ringing bell. It was definitely not Ava's own voice. "You have asked for enlightenment, Abdur Rahman, Servant of the Most Gracious, and enlightenment shall be given unto you."

She should have been scared. But the trembling in her body wasn't fear.

In her heart was a new certainty: The answers to Prince Abdur Rahman's questions could change the world. Guidance would bring peace to his heart and give him the courage to move forward. *Everything in life needs an anchor,* Granny Buena had said. This moment could be an anchor for the bright future Abdur Rahman might help build.

Abdur Rahman rose to his feet in a quick, catlike move. His gaze was awed yet joyful.

Ava smiled upon him and opened her mouth again, waiting for more miraculous words to rise to her lips. She spread her arms wide like an angel, ready for the big reveal. And . . .

Nothing happened.

She felt herself blushing as the prince and everyone else on board stared at her, waiting for the promised enlightenment.

Where had that awesome power of speech gone? And what was she supposed to do now?

Meow!

Ava felt the pricking of tiny cat claws on her leg.

She looked down, then said in her regular voice, "Oh, you've got to be kidding me." She didn't know whether to feel annoyed or relieved at the interruption, but it didn't matter because she was overcome by surprise above all.

"Sheba!" Nadeem exclaimed.

From a coil of rope where she'd been hiding, Sheba leaped up to the tiller, brushing an astonished Ester with her tail, then dropped into Ava's arms. The orange fire opal hanging from the cat's collar shone brightly. When Ava caught sight of it, she got the same hypnotized feeling she'd experienced back in Granny Buena's living room.

Snap out of it! You can't go back to your own time yet. You have something to tell the prince first!

She tried hard to focus on Abdur Rahman. But the jewel was too bright for her to resist.

Nadeem reached out to place a hand on Sheba's

head. A familiar whispery, songlike humming swirled up into the air.

Holding tight to the golden cat, Ava's gaze drifted from Ester to Prince Abdur Rahman to Bedir the Greek. When the button took her away from these amazing people, she would never see them again. Which meant she needed to speak right now, in the next few seconds. She couldn't wait any longer for inspiration. She had to do this herself.

The words on the Button Box suddenly flashed into her mind:

> *Mend hearts,*
> *and fasten together*
> *the fabric of time.*

Wait. She had it! Ava could mend the prince's heart by answering his questions about the future— because where she came from, that future had already happened. Granny had told her and Nadeem all about it!

"Prince of the Umayyads, you are rightly guided on this journey!" she cried, echoing the words he'd used earlier. "Yes, your destiny is to rule Spain! You'll make it a place where everyone worships freely. In your land, writing and reading, music and math, science and medicine will be the best in the world, because you'll welcome everyone's ideas instead of turning away people who are different from you. Your story will be handed down from generation to generation. Oh—and keep Bedir close, since he's obviously your best friend. Good job, Bedir."

There. She'd done it!

Nadeem cleared his throat to add, "And uh, Your Highness, you obviously already know this, but I guess it can't hurt to say it again. We are supposed to be open to people, no matter who they are or where they're from. Remember that verse in the Qu'ran: *O mankind, indeed We created you from a male and female and made you nations and tribes, that you may know one another.*"

Nice one, thought Ava. How did he come up with such a great word-for-word quote all of a sudden? Come to think it, the quote was even kind of familiar to her. Aha! She remembered: It was from a laminated plaque that hung by the bookshelf in Nadeem's living room. His mom had gotten it as a gift from her interfaith group.

Prince Abdur Rahman drew closer to Ava. His

compelling eyes held a fire even stronger than the light of Sheba's opal. "I hear the will of the All-Seeing, and I will do His bidding with gratitude to the end of my strength for the years, days, and hours remaining to me."

The humming sound grew louder.

The pin on Ava's robe pulled at her.

She turned to Ester ibn Evram, wishing she could give the girl a hug, but she couldn't let go of Sheba. "Ester," she said, "don't let anyone call you 'little' anymore, because you've done something huge! Your family will listen to you now. Go ahead and move to Spain, and take them all with you!"

Ester seemed unable to answer. She was shaking.

Nadeem then totally wrecked the mystical mood. "Oh yeah—in case you haven't guessed, we're family to you, Ester, but we aren't really Nathan and Abigail. They'll probably show up in Sabtah any day now and confuse your mom a *lot*."

Sheba interrupted with a loud, impatient *meow*.

The button started to vibrate, pulling harder and harder. The deck of the fishing boat tilted under Ava's feet.

She clutched Sheba closer.

"Goodbye, Ester!" she called. "Goodbye, Bedir! Goodbye—" But the boat and the people in it were growing dim, fading from view.

In the next instant, she and Nadeem found themselves back in Granny Buena's living room.

Sheba wriggled out of Ava's too-tight grip with a yowl of annoyance. She dropped to the floor and stalked away.

CHAPTER 14

When Granny Buena finally came downstairs, Ava and Nadeem were sitting quietly on the sofa.

Their math books were open. Their pencils were scratching out long division problems. The silver-and-ruby button of Ester ibn Evram and Abdur Rahman was nowhere to be seen, because it was safely back in the magnificent crystal and gold Button Box on the dining room table.

"So, ninyos, did you have a good time while I napped?" Granny asked.

Ava looked at Nadeem.

Nadeem looked at Ava.

Sheba leaped down from the top of the bookshelf where she'd been waiting and landed on Granny's shoulder. The opal on her collar was back to normal again—no glowing or anything. It swung out and hit one of Granny's necklaces with a faint chime.

"We learned a lot while you were asleep," Ava said feebly.

No way was she going to say anything about what had really happened. Granny would never believe it . . . would she? Even if she did, she'd probably lock the Button Box away forever to keep her grandchildren from taking any other dangerous trips back in time.

"Good!" said Granny. "How is your homework coming along?"

"Okay so far," said Nadeem. "We just got started."

"*Kosa empesada, es media eskapada*," Granny observed. "A task begun is already half done."

"I wish!" said Nadeem. "When we're done with this, we have to get started on a group social studies project."

Ava put down her pencil. "Nadeem and I were actually thinking we could do that project on the prince you told us about. You know . . . Abdur Rahman. And, uh, maybe that ancestor of ours, Ester ibn Evram. The one who got the button from the prince."

Sheba purred from her perch on Granny's shoulders.

Granny looked amused. "*La, la, la,* how delightful

that you're both so interested in the prince and the spice seller! I must be a much better tale-teller than I thought."

Ava chose her words carefully. "You're a great storyteller. I almost feel like I know Ester."

"I find that fascinating, my dear, since I didn't even finish the story." Granny gave her a teasing look. "We will have to find a chance to do that soon."

Nadeem's cheeks turned red. Ava figured hers were red too, because they felt hot.

Granny didn't seem to notice. She settled into a nearby armchair and crossed her legs at the ankles. Sheba lightly dropped into her lap. "So, keridos, have you decided what to do about that bully at your school? *Something* must be done. Such behavior can't be allowed to continue."

"We actually thought of a really good way to teach Fern a lesson," said Nadeem.

"Oh, yes?"

Ava explained, "We're going to ask our social studies teacher to assign Fern as our partner on this history project. That means she's going to have to interview our families about Jewish and Muslim traditions, take a bunch of notes, and do the presentations with us. It's going to be awesome!"

Granny didn't seem convinced. "Do you think that will help? It might simply make her resentful."

"Honestly, Granny, we think it's worth a try," Nadeem said. "This project could make her see us in a different way. And it might help her learn the truth about who Muslims and Jews are."

Ava put in, "Not because we're going to preach at her. But because she won't be able to help falling in love with the story of Abdur Rahman and Ester! And from there, I think we can reel her in from the Dark Side."

Granny nodded slowly. "There is great power in stories. I think you may be right."

"So is it okay if we bring her here to talk to you about our family?" Ava watched Granny Buena's face closely.

A hint of glee appeared in the green eyes. "Aha. You're asking your old granny to talk to this girl? My dears, now I feel sure that Fern will learn a great deal from this project."

Ava flipped her math book shut. "Granny, do you think I could start going to Hebrew lessons once a week with Rochelle and Eliza?"

"Going once a week, it might take you many years to learn Hebrew, my darling, but of course. I'll talk to your mother about it. And perhaps those girls might like to learn a little Ladino from you?"

Ava nodded slowly. "Maybe they would." Ava had a feeling they might also like to hear Abdur Rahman's theory about turning bystanders into heroes.

"That all sounds good to me." Nadeem shoved aside his homework and lifted his hands to Sheba, who was batting at Granny's brightly colored bead necklaces. "Here, kitty, kitty!"

Sheba considered him for a minute. Then she jumped from Granny's lap to Nadeem's.

"You're an awesome kitty," he said in a gooey voice, stroking her golden fur as if they'd always been best pals. "Such a brave kitty. So smart!" When his petting slowed down, Sheba whacked him with her paw. "Oops! Sorry." He sped up the strokes again.

Sheba purred loudly.

Over Nadeem's head, Ava caught their grandmother's eye with a smile. "*In the hands of children, there are miracles.* Right, Granny Buena?"

Granny quirked up one corner of her mouth . . . and winked.

GLOSSARY

Aleinu: "It is our duty to praise" in Hebrew, the Jewish closing prayer for morning, afternoon, and evening worship

Alhamdulilah: "praise be to God" or "thanks be to God" in Arabic, said in gratitude for a blessing

Allah: "God" in Arabic

Allahu Akbar: "God is great" in Arabic, used in prayer or in thanks

as-salaamu alaykum: "may peace be upon you" in Arabic, a traditional Muslim greeting

audhu billah: "I seek refuge in God" in Arabic

Berbers: a diverse ethnic group that has lived in North Africa since prehistoric times, thousands of years before Arabic-speaking Muslims conquered much of the region

bismillah: "in the name of God" in Arabic, said at the beginning of an undertaking, including before eating or drinking something

caliph: a Muslim religious and government leader

Hashem: "The Name," a respectful Hebrew substitute for speaking the name of God in conversation

Insh'Allah: "God willing" in Arabic

Jabal Tāriq: "Mountain of Tāriq," the Arabic name for a region on the southeastern coast of Spain that juts out into the Mediterranean Sea, also called Gibraltar

jadah: "grandma" in Arabic

kerida/kerido: "dear one" in Ladino

Ladino: a language closely related to Spanish and shaped by Hebrew, Arabic, and numerous other languages; also known as Judeo-Spanish

Mash'Allah: "what God has willed" in Arabic, used to express appreciation and a sense of wonder

mezuzah: a piece of parchment inscribed with Hebrew verses from the Torah (the first five books of the Hebrew Bible, believed to have been written by Moses) and attached to the doorpost of a Jewish home

mikvah: a pool of water used for ritual bathing in some Jewish traditions

ninya/ninyo: "girl," "boy," or "kid" in Ladino

nona: "grandma" in Ladino, as well as in Spanish. Some Ladino speakers might spell it as "nonna."

Subhan Allah: "glory be to God" in Arabic

tagine: a northwestern African stew traditionally slow-cooked in a covered earthenware pot with a cone-shaped lid; also the pot itself

tikkun olam: "repairing the world" in Hebrew, actions meant to make the world a better place

wa'alaykum as-salaam: "may peace be upon you" in Arabic, a traditional response to the Muslim greeting "as-salaamu alaykum"

AUTHORS' NOTE

Who are Sephardic Jews?

Judaism is a religion, but it is also an identity and a way of life. Jews believe in one God, the God of Abraham. According to teachings, Jewish laws were revealed by God to the prophet Moses on Mount Sinai, which scholars now think is probably the mountain of the same name located in Egypt. Judaism is the predecessor of all later "Abrahamic" religions, including Christianity and Islam. There are many ways to be Jewish, but an emphasis on good deeds, good hearts, love, family and tradition are shared by all.

Ashkenazic Jews are descended from the Jews of Eastern Europe. Most American Jews are of Ashkenazi descent.

Sephardic Jews like Granny Buena and Ava are descended from Jews who lived in Spain and Portugal beginning in ancient times. Their traditional language is Ladino—a mix of Spanish, Hebrew, Arabic, and other languages. Their traditional food can have a Mediterranean flair that often brings the flavor of lemons, apricots, almonds, tomatoes, honey, and slow-cooked meats to the table.

The Sephardic Jews didn't leave Spain until the late 1400s, when a Christian king and queen—the same people who paid for Christopher Columbus's expedition to the Americas—overthrew the Muslim leadership. They told Jews and Muslims to either convert to Catholicism—their branch of Christianity—or die. Many Jews were killed, but others managed to flee to safer places like Portugal, Brazil, and the Ottoman Empire, where Islamic Sultans ruled over parts of Europe, the Middle East, and Africa for more than six hundred years.

Author Bridget Hodder's family were among those fleeing Jews. They lived in the city of Salonica in the Ottoman Empire until World War II, when Jews once again had to run for their lives and leave their homes behind. This time they were pursued not by Spaniards but by the Nazis of Germany and their allies. Bridget's grandmother Rachel; aunt Lillian; mother, Odile; and other

Author Bridget Hodder's maternal grandparents at their wedding.
Most of the relatives in this photograph did not survive the Holocaust.

relatives escaped to the United States. Others, like her mother's grandmother Ester and her mother's aunt Buena, perished in the Nazi concentration camp at Auschwitz.

Today, Jews make up only 2 percent of the US population, but they are the targets of 60 percent of US hate crimes. That's a lot! So be an ally to your Jewish friends and neighbors—and even to Jews who are complete strangers to you. Put a stop to mean talk or cruel actions happening around you.

Who are Muslims?

Muslims practice the faith of Islam. They worship the same God worshipped by Jews. In fact, Arabic-speaking Jews and Christians in the Middle East use the Arabic word for God, Allah, just as Muslims do. Muslims believe that since the beginning of time, God has sent His message to all nations—so they see Islam as a continuation of the same message given to the Prophets Adam ﷺ, Abraham ﷺ, Moses ﷺ, and Jesus ﷺ. (This symbol is a tiny square of Arabic writing that says, "peace and blessings of God be upon him." Muslims use this phrase after the name of a messenger of God. It is a sign of love and respect.)

According to Islam, around the year 610, the Angel Gabriel ﷺ visited the Prophet Muhammad ﷺ and instructed him to say some words out loud. These words became the Holy Book the Qu'ran (or Koran). The Qur'an's message in its simplest form is that humans should do good deeds and worship no one but God. Over time, some Muslims have divided into different groups like Sunnis and Shi-ites, but most followers of Islam prefer to call themselves simply Muslims. Muslim places of worship are called mosques.

There are over 1.25 billion Muslims in the world today. In the United States, they make up only about 1 percent of the population. Still, they are targets of at least 20 percent of the hate crimes committed in the United States. So being an ally and looking out for your Muslim friends and neighbors is very important. If people insult or threaten Muslims while you're around, step in. Speak up. And tell a trusted adult.

Was Prince Abdur Rahman real?

There really was a Prince Abdur Rahman, and his tutor, Bedir, was real too! Abdur Rahman's name can be spelled many different ways, including *Abd al-Rahman*, which is how you should Google him if you're looking for more information. (And we hope you are!) The prince was born in Syria in 731 CE. As a young man, he was forced to flee his home when the Umayyad royal family was overthrown by the Abbasids. In 755, he reached Al-Andalus in what is now Spain, and soon afterward he became the region's ruler.

The nation known today as Spain didn't yet exist. The ancient Romans called it Hispania, the Arabs called it Al-Andalus, and the Jews of Spain

The mosque built by Abdur Rahman's family in Damascus, Syria, is still one of the great wonders of the Muslim world.

and Portugal called it Sepharad—which is the reason they were known as Sephardic Jews. To keep it simple, the region is called Spain in this book. The ancient town of Sabtah is now called Ceuta, and even though it is located across the Mediterranean sea from Europe, it is officially part of Spain.

Abdur Rahman's reign lasted more than thirty years. His people included Muslims, Jews, and Christians. His capital city of Córdoba was so lovely that it became known as "the ornament of the world." The city still exists, and so does the Great Mosque that Abdur Rahman and his people built.

Abdur Rahman's descendants ruled a broad region including all of Spain and part of what is now France. Their rule, known as Spain's "Golden Age," ended in the 1400s, when Catholic Christian forces overthrew them and banished Muslims and Jews from the beautiful lands they loved.

Did Ester ibn Evram really help Abdur Rahman escape North Africa?

History tells us that *somebody* helped Abdur Rahman escape with his tutor, Bedir, while greedy crowds tried to stop them. But the names of those who helped are lost in the mists of time.

Ester ibn Evram and her family are fictional characters. However, Jews like them did live in North Africa in the year 755. So even if the prince and Bedir's crossing to Spain didn't happen exactly as it does in this book . . . it *could* have happened that way.

That's what fiction is all about. Use your imagination while you read real history, and you can put yourself right in the middle of its most exciting events!

Until our next adventure into the past—*Shalom, Salaam!*

ACKNOWLEDGMENTS

We relied on several excellent resources for the history surrounding this book, especially *The Ornament of the World: How Muslims, Jews, and Christians Created a Culture of Tolerance in Medieval Spain* by María Rosa Menocal. Another valuable resource for adults about the interactions between Muslims and Jews is *A History of Jewish-Muslim Relations: From the Origins to the Present Day*, edited by Abdelwahab Meddeb and Benjamin Stora.

Bridget and Fawzia would like to thank Joni Sussman, who believed in this book from the very beginning and who introduced us to each other. We're also deeply grateful to Amy Fitzgerald for her inspired and inspiring editing skills, to incredibly gifted illustrator Harshad Marathe, to creative director Emily Harris, and to the rest of the Lerner team. We are grateful as well to Catriella Friedman and the PJ Our Way review committee who helped with early drafts of this book. Thanks are also due to PJ Library and the Harold Grinspoon Foundation for their Author Incentive Award which supported the writing of *The Button Box*. We greatly appreciate the further wise counsel and input of Dr. Freda Shamma; Victoria J. Coe; Joan Paquette; Laura Shovan; and Carolyn Schwartz. Note, however, that any mistakes or missteps in this work are solely the responsibility of the authors, not our helpful friends.

I dedicate my share of this book with love to my father, David Hodder, who left this earth in 2021; may his name become a blessing to his descendants. And to my dear lifelong friend Carla, a Sephardic sister whom I also lost during the writing of this book, and her twin sister Diana. To my husband and family, who support me in every way that counts. Lastly, I want to thank my coauthor, who has dedicated her life to faith and peace, Fawzia Gilani-Williams. Fawzia, it's been a joy to share this work of love with such a sensitive, wonderful writer . . . and to be able to call you friend.

—Bridget Hodder

~Bismillah~ Dear Lord, I thank you first for everything. Thank you, dear Bridget, my sister-friend—you are a passionate peacemaker and interfaith bridge builder, alhamdulilah! You have been the lead in this beautiful project that empowers children to take action against bullying and hatefulness. We need more heroes! God bless you!

—Fawzia Gilani-Williams

ABOUT THE AUTHORS

Bridget Hodder is a historian and archaeologist as well as an author. *The Button Box* is her second middle-grade novel; she is also the author of *The Rat Prince*. She lives in New England.

Fawzia Gilani-Williams is an international educational consultant and the author of many children's books, including *A Treasury of Eid Tales*, and the picture book *Yaffa and Fatima*. She spends her time in the United Arab Emirates, Ohio, and England with her daughter and husband.